"What did you plan for later, Clare?"

Macey's jaw was tightened in anger. "Dinner here, and then what...?"

A burning flush ran up Clare's face. "I don't know what you're talking about!" she cried.

Macey took a step nearer. His face was suffused with color, his lips grim. "You know what I'm talking about."

She backed away, her eyes shifting. "I don't."

"The answer is no, Clare. I don't want you using me to get yourself over the shock of seeing Luke again."

"I was doing nothing of the kind," she retorted furiously.

"Oh, yes," he grated, anger making him seem taller and more powerful than ever. "Do you think I'm too stupid to catch on?"

I'm the one who's stupid, Clare thought helplessly, *to have ever let myself near Luke....*

CHARLOTTE LAMB

is also the author of these

Harlequin Presents

and these

Harlequin Romances

CHARLOTTE LAMB

stranger in the night

Harlequin Books

TORONTO • LONDON • LOS ANGELES • AMSTERDAM
SYDNEY • HAMBURG • PARIS • STOCKHOLM • ATHENS • TOKYO

Harlequin Presents edition published March 1981
ISBN 0-373-10417-0

Original hardcover edition published in 1980
by Mills & Boon Limited

Printed in U.S.A.

CHAPTER ONE

It was around half-past eleven that Clare lost sight of Leonie. The room was so overcrowded that it was hard to see anyone except those nearest to you. Clare had been dancing with a large young man in an improbable fuzzy orange sweater, whose hands gripped her far too tightly, and who was too drunk for her to be able to understand a word he said. When the music stopped he let go of her and she was swept away from him in a surge of people. She wasn't sorry to see the last of him. Edging her way with difficulty to the wall, she stood on tiptoes to peer over heads in an effort to catch a glimpse of Leonie's red hair. Surely Leonie wouldn't have left?

Clare's heart sank at the thought. She didn't know a single soul at this party except Leonie. Someone had lowered the lights earlier and on the outskirts of the room ran a rim of dark shadow in which she hovered, like a disembodied spirit, anxiously scanning half-seen faces in the crowd.

She had never been to a party like this one before—a rather young eighteen, straight up from the country, her big green eyes still wide and innocent, her previous ideas of parties had faded tonight into dim insignificance.

Leonie had flung her into a host of strangers to sink

or swim, and Clare had been making a brave effort to swim, but now she felt horribly lonely and deserted.

The glittering blue dress she was wearing was not her own. Leonie had smuggled her stage costume out of the theatre, against all the rules, shrugging with a smile when Clare protested.

'Go ahead! Try it on! After all, who'll know? As long as it's back in the dressing-room tomorrow it won't matter. And you can't go to a flash New Year's Eve party in a pair of shabby old jeans.'

Looking in the mirror later Clare had been too tempted by the sight of herself in the dress to be able to refuse the offered loan.

'It suits you down to the ground,' Leonie had told her. 'Better than it does me.'

Leonie looked good in anything, but the blue shade of the dress did not quite agree with Leonie's red hair. She looked better in the black dress she had made herself. It had made Clare's eyes grow round and incredulous. What there had been of it had been daring and chic—and Clare had known that she would never be able to wear such clothes. Leonie had clever hands. She often helped out in the wardrobe, making costumes. Slim, vivacious, Leonie was friendly and kind in a casual, half-taunting fashion. She made no secret of the fact that Clare's breathless, romantic innocence amused her. Leonie was doing her best to help Clare grow up. 'We must bring you up to date,' she had said bluntly. 'We're in the nineteen-eighties now, remember. You're not a schoolgirl any more.'

Clare had been brought up in a quiet little town

which seemed to die at six o'clock. London was still a dazzling revelation to her. The last thing she wanted was to be laughed at, so she had listened, impressed, eager to learn the sophistication Leonie seemed to wear so lightly.

Leonie lived in the same house, a ramshackle old London terraced house split into one-room apartments, run by a garrulous and sociable old theatrical dresser called Hilda, whose flat feet were never seen in anything but carpet slippers.

'Me feet's ruined, ducks,' she used to tell them, sighing. 'That's what the theatre did for me.' Her eye would roll wickedly at them. 'Ruined, I was.'

Leonie encouraged her to tell them reminiscences of theatre life forty years ago. Hilda loved having people from the profession living in her house. She was maternal and warm-hearted, very tolerant, leaving them alone so long as they didn't take what she called 'liberties', which meant in general that they paid their rent on time and did not throw wild parties in their rooms or have young men in them at night.

Clare had been lucky to find such a good place. The rent was reasonable. It was clean and as comfortable as one could expect. It was as much as she could afford. The money her parents gave her only stretched to the barest essentials, and she had already lost five pounds since coming to London. She had learnt to skip meals and exist on bread and baked beans. In her first year at a drama school she was finding life very exciting and very difficult.

Leonie had a job in the chorus of an out-of-town

show. She had slightly more money than Clare, but she spent more.

The whole cast had been invited to this party by one of the stars. Clare did not even know where they were—she had been swept up into the noisy, excited group, but she had no idea who her companions were, except that Leonie had muttered a few first names at her as people smiled at her.

Clare had already drunk more than she had ever drunk in her life before. Her previous acquaintance with drink had run to one sherry now and then, but tonight people had pressed glasses into her hand and she had absently emptied them. Now she was feeling distinctly odd—not drunk, she told herself, just light-headed. She had only eaten beans on toast again today and whisky was doing something strange to her metabolism.

There was no sign of Leonie's red head anywhere. Clare moved away, frowning anxiously.

She ought to leave, she told herself, wondering how she was going to get back to her flat at this hour. She would never get a taxi.

'Hallo, Charleston girl!'

The husky voice at her side startled her. She whirled, the beaded fringe of her short dress flaring round her knees.

'You're not dancing! We can't have that. That dress was made for dancing in, wasn't it?' The tall man who had materialised beside her slid his arm round her waist and smiled at her.

Clare laughed with the light sophistication she was

imitating from Leonie, flicking her long, darkened lashes up and then down again.

'Have we met?'

The stranger laughed. 'We have now,' he pointed out in what she suddenly recognised as an American accent.

'Are you an American?'

'Yes,' he said, smiling. 'And you're English. A typical English rose.' His glance slid down her slender, curved body in the daring little metallic blue dress. Armless, low-necked, it left little of her to the imagination. Leonie's musical was set in the nineteen-twenties, but the costume deliberately had a modernity which lent Clare a deceptive sophistication. Somehow the very feel of the costume taught her to move with audacity.

Her hair was a natural honey blonde, warm and smooth, styled for simplicity, since she could not afford to visit a hairdresser and had to look after it herself. It fell to her shoulders in a straight, golden curtain which swished as she turned her head to smile at her new acquaintance.

She was very conscious of the flattery his eyes were offering her as he took in her appearance, and a faint flush rose into her cheeks.

'I don't think I've ever met an American before.'

'What a confession!' His voice teased and his eyes mocked. 'Time you got to know one, then.'

'You?' Clare opened her eyes wide, their soft misty green gleaming between those dark lashes, and he looked into them with an amused glint.

'Me, Charleston girl.'

He drew her into his arms and they moved in among the other dancers. They were soon so close that she could feel every movement he made, his arms tightly wrapped around her, his thighs sliding against hers. He was a tall, slim man with wide shoulders and an elegantly proportioned body under the dark evening suit he wore. She looked at it, recognising vaguely that it had an expensive cut and styling, which must mean that he wasn't in anything like her own income bracket.

'You're very elegant,' she said brightly. 'Have you been anywhere special?'

'Not until now,' he said, his smile underlining the flattery.

Clare laughed, beginning to feel strangely excited. She had never met anyone like him in her life and her heart had begun to beat rather alarmingly. He was not only outside her income bracket; he was out of her age group, too, she realised. It was hard to tell in the muted light, but she suspected he was much closer to thirty than twenty, and his sophistication was genuine, unlike her own imitated variety.

The faint frisson of doubt which ran down her spine was dispelled by another of his charming little smiles. Clare was fascinated by those smiles. The grey eyes mocked and invited, the mouth curved upward with amusement.

He's a very sexy man, she thought, tingling with excitement. She thought of what she would tell Leonie, her eyes dancing. Leonie had a way of making patronising little digs which got under Clare's skin. It would be satisfying to show Leonie how wrong she was—

none of the men Leonie went around with was as sexy as this man.

'You go around like one of the babes in the wood,' Leonie had said in a derisive voice earlier that evening.

Clare was going to show her a thing or two.

'You dance as beautifully as I thought you would, Charleston girl,' her partner said softly against her ear. She felt his mouth slide over her lobe, and quivered.

He laughed softly, as though that involuntary and betraying tremor in her body had delighted him.

The music came to an end, but he kept his arm wrapped around her. Someone passed around champagne. Whoever was giving this party had a lot of money, Clare noted interestedly, drinking her champagne with enthusiasm. The bubbles prickled in her nose and she sneezed. Her companion laughed and reached a long arm over to get her another glass.

'I don't even know your name,' she said as she accepted it without a qualm.

'Luke,' he said. 'What's yours, Charleston girl?'

'Clare.'

There was a blast of toy trumpets as some new revellers swept into the already crowded room. The crowd swayed back and forth like a live thing and Luke drew Clare closer. Someone shouted that it was almost midnight. The room hushed, and everyone began to count aloud in unison. 'Five-four-three-two-one ... Happy New Year!'

There was a roar of voices. Laughter followed it, then people awkwardly linked hands with those around them to sing Auld Lang Syne in a ragged enthusiasm which made the words barely intelligible.

Clare had finished her second glass of champagne. The dancing began again and she found herself crushed so tightly against Luke that she was aware of every inch of his body. She lowered her hectically flushed face to his shoulder, her arms around his neck, and felt his hand pressing along her spine, fondling her in a leisurely exploration which increased the pace of her heartbeat.

Suddenly he paused to whisper: 'I've had enough of this—have you? Shall we go?'

Clare was feeling particularly sleepy. The slow shuffling of their bodies, the heat in the room, the muffled beat of the music had made her head heavy. The champagne hadn't helped either, she thought. It had apparently got into her bloodstream and was bubbling through her and making her head swim.

She wasn't beyond common sense, however. 'Go where?' she asked suspiciously, lifting her head from his shoulder.

'Let's find a quieter party,' Luke said lightly. 'There are too many people at this one.'

Clare frowned, trying to focus on him. 'Do you know a quieter party?'

'I do, Charleston girl.' He smiled down into her dreamy green eyes and Clare smiled back.

'Good thinking!'

'I hoped you'd say that,' he told her with amusement.

He forced a passage through the overcrowded room,

pulling her after him by the wrist. A few young men tried to detain her, kissing her with noisy enthusiasm, and Luke detached her from them calmly. She had forgotten all about Leonie. She followed Luke like a lost traveller following a will-o'-the-wisp over marshy ground, struggling after him, elbows digging into her, feet trampling on her toes.

The party was being held in one of a large block of expensive apartments in St John's Wood. As they dived out of the door they ran full tilt into a group of new arrivals blowing squeakers and singing. Clare let Luke pull her through them and as last found herself safely in the elevator.

She leaned on the wall, her stomach suddenly heaving. The motion of the elevator made her dizzy. Am I drunk? she asked herself, her eyes closed.

The elevator stopped. Luke guided her out of it and propped her against the wall. She leaned there, eyes closed, breathing cooler air, feeling the tremendous relief of the silence.

Luke put an arm around her again and she opened her eyes to find herself being steered into another apartment. It was very quiet.

Clare frowned and looked up at him enquiringly. 'Where are we? Where's the party?'

'In here,' said Luke, laughing.

She let him walk into the room and then stopped, realising it was empty. A surge of panic hit her and she turned in protest.

'You said . . .'

Luke's arms went round her before she could finish

the sentence. His mouth found hers and the warm, sensual movement of it took her by surprise. She barely knew what she was doing, her lips parting on instinct, as though men as sophisticated and sexy as this kissed her every day of her life.

It wasn't her first kiss. That had happened four years ago, when she was fourteen, and she had been very disappointed in it at the time. The boy had been a mature fifteen, a hero to the whole school because he had built himself a motorbike from scrap. It didn't have an engine, but he kept it in his garden and was to be admired seated on it every evening after school. All the girls were in love with him. When he kissed Clare she had expected some miraculous transformation to take place, but it had been a disillusioning experience.

She had been kissed since, of course, but none of them had ever done a thing to her.

As Luke sensitively moulded her mouth with his own, she felt her ears begin to drum and her heart to race vividly.

It was all that she had imagined a kiss would be when she was fourteen years old. When his tongue tip touched her inner lip she almost fainted with pleasure.

He ran his fingers into her full soft hair and tilted her head backwards, bringing his mouth down hard on her own, the pressure and demand of the kiss deepening.

Clare slid closer. Her excitement became intense. She slid her arms round his neck and stroked and ruffled his thick dark hair, and she felt him tense at her touch.

He broke off the kiss to look down at her with half-closed eyes, and Clare languidly moved her hand to trace the handsome lines of his face, her fingers delicately picking out his cheekbones, his mouth.

She had forgotten about the party he had said they were going to—her mind was swamped by the rush of sensual experience which was so new to her.

Their eyes held and her heart thudded at the excitement in his eyes. He began to kiss her again, and she felt his hand moving down her hip. He moved closer and the long body was hard and tense. She heard the fierce intake of his breath.

He drew back again, a dark flush on his cheekbones, his eyes glittering as he stared down at her. 'Come on, honey,' he said unevenly. 'We aren't going to stand here all night, are we?'

Dimly Clare thought he was talking about the party they were supposed to be going to and she frowned. Her head was spinning. She couldn't take her eyes off the handsome face looking down at her. Staring at the sensual line of his mouth, she marvelled at the effect it was having on her. She wanted him to kiss her again. Curving an arm round his neck, she told him so drowsily, her voice trembling.

'You're lovely,' he whispered, kissing her again.

She clung to his mouth like an addict, shivering, one hand against his cheek.

'I don't want to go to the party,' she muttered thickly, and Luke laughed under his breath.

'This party is just for two, darling.'

Before she had time to consider what that meant, he had slid his hands under her back and knees, and lifted her into his arms. Her head went round. It fell against his shoulder, feeling the muscles in it flex as he carried her out of the room.

It was dark in the corridor. Clare's eyes shut and she felt she was falling, her mind totally at sea. She tried to rouse herself enough to ask him were they were going, but she was too sleepy. She felt like a baby in his arms. She felt weak and warm and blissful.

He laid her down and she curled up like a child, already half asleep. She felt a movement beside her. Someone was delicately moving her. An arm was beneath her, lowering her zip.

'So sleepy,' she protested, trying to force her eyes open.

Her dress rustled down and that woke her up slightly. She opened her eyes and saw Luke's dark head above her.

'You're not drunk, are you, Charleston girl?' he asked with that little smile which had turned her head earlier.

'I feel strange,' she breathed. She lifted her hand languidly and stroked his hard-boned face. His skin was faintly rough along the jaw. He kissed her palm as she touched his mouth.

'Do you believe in love at first sight?' she asked in a sleepy voice.

'Do you, Charleston girl?'

She frowned as she suddenly realised he was undoing his shirt, and a flash of anxiety went through her. 'What are you doing?'

He stopped unbuttoning the shirt and took her

flushed face between his hands. 'What do you think I'm doing, darling?' Before she could answer that he began to kiss her again, and Clare floated away on a tide of physical pleasure which was totally new to her.

I'm in love, she thought dreamily. It was all true, all the myths and fables about love. The heart did beat faster—hers was beating like a drunken metronome. The breath did come irregularly; she could scarcely breathe at all. A kiss could be heaven, and all the times when she had rebelliously let someone kiss her only to decide it had all been a boring waste of time, she just hadn't been kissing the right person. She was kissing him now and he was making her whole body melt and burn.

While he was kissing her, however, Luke was deftly doing a number of other things without Clare being aware of it at first. It was only as she suddenly realised that they were both naked and that Luke's hands were moving in a slow, sensual exploration of her body that she snapped out of her dazed mood.

'No!' she gasped, pulling away and trying to push his hands down. 'You mustn't!'

'Don't play games, Charleston girl,' he muttered thickly.

Clare wasn't playing games. She was filling with panic as she felt his long fingers possessing her body.

'I can't,' she whispered shakily. 'Luke, please don't!'

He had cupped her breasts, and a piercing sexual excitement swept through her. It was her first experience of such intense physical feeling and she drew in her breath on a fierce gasp. Luke laughed softly and his fingers teased and incited her response.

Her breasts were aching, hardening, the smooth white flesh abruptly heating and swelling.

She began to whisper pleadingly, her voice shaking, but Luke wasn't even listening. She saw his face in the darkness. He looked different suddenly: harder, more masculine, the smile completely gone. He was stroking her breasts and staring and she could hear the sharp, harsh sound of his breathing.

He looked up at her as she stopped speaking on a painful breath, his eyes glittering in the darkness. Clare forgot everything. She was held in a strange, suspended limbo, drowning in the intent hard stare of his eyes.

It was then that real fear flared inside her head. The euphoria induced by all the drink she had consumed went so suddenly that she felt sick, but she was wide awake now, and terrified.

'I've never . . .' she began huskily, and was cut short by the bruising, fierce demand of his mouth. He was fondling her thighs, his body moving against her, holding her so that she couldn't escape.

'No,' she moaned under his mouth.

'What do you mean, no?' He lifted his head and that charming mouth looked as though it had never worn a smile in its life. His face was deeply flushed and savage. His lips curled back and she saw white teeth clenched together. 'I don't like girls who tease,' he muttered, barely parting his teeth to speak. 'I'm in no mood for games now. You've had your fun, now I want mine.'

She went into a frenzy of panic, struggling violently,

hitting him with flailing hands which had no idea how to cope with his superior strength, clawing down his face as she fought to get away. She felt her nails raking his skin and he swore with a savagery that appalled her.

'You little bitch!'

Her scream split the silent apartment. His body violently invaded hers and his hand clamped down over her mouth as she went on crying out in wounded protest.

She went on struggling wildly to escape the pain he was inflicting on her, icy fear making her cold from head to foot, her brain now very clear and stricken with misery, but he ignored her muffled cries, the hands pushing at his broad, naked shoulders, the damp palms sliding on his skin.

When he finally lay still beside her, Clare was trembling, her ears still aching with the sound of his pleasure, sickness cramping her stomach.

She felt him turn over on his side without a word and a few moments later she realised he was asleep, breathing heavily, one arm flung out above his dark head.

She waited tensely, like a frightened little animal, her brain reeling under the impact of what had happened to her. It had all been a mad, surrealist nightmare—the party, the strangers, the drink to which she was so unaccustomed, the feeling of being alone in strange territory.

In the dark room she became aware of the faint odour of whisky hanging around him. He had been drinking, too, although she had never noticed because she had been half drunk herself.

She ran her cold, trembling hands over her face. She had to get away while he was asleep. She couldn't face him in the morning; she winced at the thought of how he would look at her, what he would say. She didn't want anyone looking at her. She felt unclean and sick.

Luke had thought she was used to being picked up like that. She realised now just what sort of girl he had thought she was, shame burning in her face. Through the darkness she stared at the wide, bare shoulders, the long smooth spine.

He had brought her here with him, believing her to be available, imagining that she knew precisely what was in his mind. The wild emotions she had been feeling had never entered his head. He had picked up a girl for the night, and that was all there was to it on his side.

Her breathless dream of a sudden, fateful love had all been moonshine. The sickness in her grew, eating at her. How could she have been so stupid? Her own innocence had betrayed her into his hands and she was torn between hating herself and hating him.

He had gone through a charade of love for her that night, whispering sweet words, kissing her with a pretence of tenderness that mocked her now. She had blindly believed he felt as she did—that he was as suddenly, blissfully involved with her as she had been with him from that first moment. She had been cheated by her own innocence and folly into believing that a sordid little one-night stand was the coming of true love.

He used me, she thought, staring at his hard, handsome profile. She slid off the bed as slowly and carefully as she could and began to dress with hands that shook.

When at last she was fully dressed again she looked down at his sleeping face. She would remember him; all her life she would remember him with hatred.

Quietly she tiptoed to the door. As she opened it, it creaked, and the little sound disturbed him. He stirred, the black head moving restlessly on the pillow, and rolled over, his body turning in a graceful movement that held her eyes. His arm fell heavily across the bed, his hand moving as though he searched for something.

Clare held her breath, trembling. The last thing she wanted was to have Luke wake up now and look at her. Now that she knew precisely what he thought of her she couldn't wait to get out of here.

Oh, God, she thought, if I'd only realised last night what it was he wanted! I don't even know his full name, she realised, with a sick qualm. Luke was all she would remember him as, and she knew that name would always make her want to throw up.

She had believed herself to be in love with a nameless stranger who had only wanted a girl in his bed for one night of enjoyment. It would be branded inside her for the rest of her life, and there was nothing she could do to remove that shame now.

Luke lay still again, his breathing loud in the quiet room. Clare softly tiptoed out and crept like a mouse down the dark corridor. She went down in the elevator and the block of apartments was totally silent now. The uproar of the night before had evaporated. In the foyer lay a tattered trail of bright red tinsel. She averted her eyes from it, wincing.

She shivered as she stepped out into the cold morning. She was given one piece of luck, anyway. A cruising taxi passed a moment later and she hailed it. The weary driver gave her a sardonic grin. 'Happy New Year, darling. Good party?'

Clare looked at him with a white face and darkened eyes and he stared back at her in surprise. 'Here, you all right, miss?'

She pulled herself together with a struggle. A stiff smile mocked her bruised mouth, but it convinced the driver. 'I'm a bit ...'

He didn't let her finish. 'Morning after the night before, eh? I know the feeling.'

Do you? she wondered. I doubt it. Only a woman who's made a complete fool of herself could come anywhere near guessing how I feel.

He dropped her outside her lodgings, brushing aside the tip she offered. 'My pleasure, darling. I'm going home now myself. It's been a busy night.'

Clare laughed wildly and he gave her another puzzled, curious look. She went slowly into the house. It was very quiet. Everyone was flat out this morning after a hectic night. She let herself into her room and sat down on the bed, dropping her head into her hands.

I'm a stupid fool, she thought savagely. In the cold, quiet first light of that new year she faced the fact that she would never be the same again. In one night she had had lessons she would never forget. They had been given by a man wanting only a brief, sensual pleasure with a girl whose name he didn't even know and for whom he felt nothing but a passing lust.

She had brought it all about herself, though. Her own behaviour at that party had made him imagine that she knew what he wanted and was offering him exactly that.

She felt a bitter anger rising inside her. He had been a dream come true, and now that dream lay in a thousand icy fragments around her feet.

In future she would guard herself against the sort of romantic folly which had led her into that bedroom and that man's possessing arms. She would never again let herself be trapped by her own heart.

I'll never feel anything again, she thought savagely. From now on I'll keep a damned great wall round myself. I'll never let myself in for this sort of pain again.

CHAPTER TWO

SUNLIGHT danced and spun in a blinding brilliance across the blue water. White sails moved languidly like distant butterflies. A plane flew low on landing course for Nice airport and Clare watched it lazily, one arm flung in a graceful curve over her head. Her nostrils picked up the delicious scent of coffee from the low, white house behind her, and closer than that, the heavy sweet scent of roses and bougainvillea, their smooth, fleshy petals closely interwoven as they crowded along the terraced levels of the garden.

Two olive trees clung to a corner of the house, their twisted shapes tormented by winter winds into beseeching gestures, the dark shade they gave during sunlight hours moving on the grass as the wind blew softly from the sea.

'Coffee, darling!' Macey said behind her, startling her.

Clare dropped her huge green sunglasses to peer at him. 'Did you have to go to Brazil to pick the beans?'

'No sarcasm at this time of the morning,' he said, his mouth twitching at one corner. As he bent to place the tray on the table, his thick dark hair fell forwards, obscuring the strong profile. Clare leaned over to brush it back and Macey gave her a hard grin.

He poured the coffee and sat down beside her, stretching his long bare legs with a contented sigh. 'This is the life! Why don't we stay here for good?'

'We can't afford to,' Clare pointed out. 'Well, I can't—you may be able to.'

The sun struck over his skin, giving it a smooth golden texture like oiled silk, as he reached for his cup. He sipped his coffee, staring at the sky, and Clare watched him, thinking that his lean, fit body performed every action with a fluid grace that caught and held the eye. Macey looked good whatever he was doing, whatever he was wearing.

He abruptly turned his head and caught her staring. A brief, sardonic glint showed in his eyes, then he smiled. 'Day-dreaming?'

'I feel disinclined to do anything,' she admitted,

lying back with her arms curved over her head.

Macey ran his glance down the rounded curve of her body, gave her a wicked leer. 'You don't have to do a thing, darling. Just lie there and let me watch you. That ravishing figure will keep me occupied all day.'

'Flattery?' Her green eyes held amusement.

'It never comes amiss,' he agreed, his eyes mocking. 'And you love it.'

'How true,' Clare admitted, laughing. 'Even when there's motive in your madness.'

'Is my play boring you to tears?' He said it smilingly, but she saw his eyes shoot sideways, very quickly, at the script she held open on her lap.

'I haven't finished it yet,' she told him firmly. 'Drink your coffee and shut up.'

'Yes, ma'am,' he muttered, picking up his cup.

It was good, she thought, her eyes flicking back to the page. She had felt the prickle on the back of her neck which told her it was good. Macey was a clever writer. His plays had an open feeling to them, a freedom which left much of the responsibility on the actors, the lines two-edged and ambiguous, so that all the meaning lay in the acting. All the best playwrights had been actors, Clare told herself. It took an actor to be aware of both the pitfalls and the possibilities of a play, to capitalise on their own professional skills so that they could construct well-shaped vehicles for fellow actors.

The levels of meaning in Macey's plays were multitude. This one could be read purely as entertainment, a commercial vehicle which she saw was bound to be highly popular, but he had fed other things into it, using that gift of ambiguity to enrich and deepen the text.

Although she knew him so well, she realised how much of Macey was still veiled to her. He was not an easy personality. Outwardly, he was an extrovert: charming, lively, good company. His plays revealed a very different man.

She had known him now for seven years. They had met while she was in her final year at drama school. Macey had been acting with a northern repertory group. An old student of the drama school, he had called in to see the end-of-term performance in which Clare had had a starring role, and he had buttonholed her afterwards to tell her that she had missed a vital chance during her performance.

Clare had prickled at the sight of him. Macey's long, lean body and dark hair resurrected memories which still had the power to make her hair bristle on the back of her neck.

Macey took no notice of her cold manner, beginning to talk at once, and his interested, serious face had impressed her enough for her to listen with growing respect.

'They didn't laugh when you threw that book because they couldn't see your face. You didn't turn towards them as you threw it, and they weren't sure if it was meant to be funny or not.'

'But the lines!' she had protested, and he had shaken his head.

'Lines can mean anything. It all depends how they're said. You fluffed the lines, took them too fast, and with your head turned away half the meaning was lost. They needed to see your face.'

She had considered that with a frown, nodding. When they had been introduced she had been told he had just had his first play performed, and that had impressed her. When Macey asked her to have supper with him, she had accepted. As they walked out of the school he grinned at her and said: 'It will have to be a scratch supper, I'm afraid. I'm skint.'

Clare had laughed. She had laughed even more as she found herself having egg and chips in a cheap café under one of London's bridges. They had argued vehemently across the plastic-topped table until an old man in a filthy raincoat leaned across to give them his own viewpoint. Cheerfully, Macey had included him in the conversation, and then the proprietor had come from behind his counter to lean on a chair and join in the discussion.

It had been a noisy, exciting evening, and very typical of Macey, whose interest in people was wide and all-embracing, whose warmth was as much a lure as a fire on a cold night and who had no barriers which excluded anyone from the circle of his friendship.

His kindness extended beyond the ordinary generosity to friends. He would give his last penny to a stranger who needed it. He loved to talk shop, as ready to learn as he was to instruct, his profession fascinating him as much as it fascinated her. She was soon very aware that Macey was far cleverer than she would ever be—but he wore his intellect lightly, disguising it from most people under the charm of his quick smile.

In the years since they met, Macey had risen like a

shooting star, largely because he wrote plays which were riveting theatre and easily produced. Two of them had been made into highly successful films. The thin young man she had met that first night had become an internationally known celebrity, but he had not changed an inch towards her.

During the first year of their friendship Macey had several times tried to deepen their easy relationship into something very different, and Clare had firmly made it clear she could not accept anything but friendship from him.

Macey was too clever not to realise she meant it. Gradually he had ceased to show her anything but casual warmth. It had been a relief to her that he accepted the situation. When Macey fell in love with someone else, Clare was ready to listen and advise him. When he rapidly fell out of love again she was ready to console and commiserate.

The pattern of their relationship had set during that first year. When Clare left drama school, Macey got her a job with the repertory company for which he was working. She had been a very junior stage manager, understudying some parts, walking on in others. It proved eventful for her when she spent the entire performance of one play lying in a deck chair wearing a tiny bikini. The audience loved it, but more importantly, a London agent had turned up to see it.

He had been visiting his aged, and irritable, mother, and had brought her to the theatre in a desperate act of boredom.

Harry Stein had brought his mother backstage afterwards. A tiny, white-haired lady of eighty, she had sat in the only chair in the cramped little dressing-room, sucking her teeth while she stared disapprovingly at the girls sharing Clare's space and chattering as they removed their make-up.

Harry Stein had ignored them, concentrating on Clare. 'You've got something,' he told her. 'I can find work for you if you come to London.'

She had been over the moon. Macey had frowned, later, saying slowly: 'Watch him, darling. He may not be interested in your acting ability.' A flick of his blue eyes had expanded that drily as he looked her over. 'You have quite a bit of ability in other directions, especially when you're only wearing a bikini.'

Clare had given him a brief, hard smile. 'Don't worry, I'm not as gullible as all that.'

Macey's eyes had watched her shrewdly, intently. 'No,' he agreed on a flat note.

She had grown up rapidly, painfully, during one night years ago, and the lessons she had learnt then had been burnt into her brain. The searing stamp had not diminished over the years. Clare carried it like a scar which could not be seen, a deep intense resistance to being used by anyone, fending off emotional involvement fiercely.

She knew she could cope with Harry Stein. He had, in fact, proved no better and no worse than Macey had predicted. Harry had attempted for a while to talk her into bed, promising her the moon, and Clare had stubbornly, coldly resisted. Harry hadn't held it against her. Shrugging wryly, he had accepted her refusals at

last and gone ahead to get her work wherever he could.
She had come to be quite fond of Harry in the end. He
had built her career with great care and energy. Her
resistance to him had impressed him, and not much
impressed Harry.

It was rumoured that he never smiled because he
had bad teeth but was too mean to spend money having
them fixed. Clare knew that was a lie. Harry had teeth,
all right, she told Macey.

'And he'd love to get them into you,' Macey had
agreed, mocking her. 'I believe they're made of gold,
anyway. If Harry goes, his money is going with him.'

Morose, shrewd, clever, Harry had been as much a
factor in her career as Macey.

She and Macey had kept in touch over the years.
They were neither of them great letter-writers, but
somehow Macey always found her, wherever she was,
dropping in casually without warning from time to
time, his casual charming smile always the same.

Their careers moved upwards at different paces, in
parallel lines which oddly crossed now and then, bringing them back together.

Macey learnt from each success, each failure, using
the lessons to enrich the next play. He was a professional to his fingertips, always looking for new ways to
hook an audience and keep them in their seats.

When one of his plays was televised he got Clare a
small part in it and they lunched together while the
rehearsals and filming went on, and when Macey had a
lead in a London production of his next play, Clare was
appearing in a short season of Ibsen at the next theatre.

They often met during that time. She had played the daughter in *The Wild Duck*, stumbling around the stage poignantly as a child going slowly blind while lost in the cruelties of an adult world she could not understand, at the mercy of people she loved and who she thought loved her until the veil was ripped from her eyes.

Clare had found the part deeply moving. It had got her a cluster of generous reviews and led directly to the part which had really brought her fame. She had got the star role in a hugely successful film and she had made a lot of money, as well as a name.

'But it wasn't acting,' she had told Macey.

He had given her his wicked smile. 'I know what it was, darling, and you looked devastating. What was it like having the great star make love to you?'

'Fine in the mornings, but he would eat garlic for lunch,' she had retorted.

Macey had roared, his blue eyes brilliant. 'You acid little realist, are there no stars in your eyes?'

She had opened her huge, glimmering green eyes at him. 'You tell me!'

Macey had moved closer, looking down into them. His hands had come up and caught her shoulders and Clare had felt an odd flicker of alarm at something in his eyes, then he had drawn back, smiling wryly. 'No,' he had agreed. 'Not a twinkle.'

The famous name playing opposite to her in the film had been less amused. When Clare coolly repulsed all his highly publicised advances, he became petulant. The handsome face which made a million hearts beat faster took on a distinctly sullen look. He was used to easy conquests and Clare's resistance infuriated him.

'You frigid little bitch,' he snapped, glaring at her during one tempestuous encounter, and Clare had laughed at the incredulous, sulky look on his face.

'Everyone expects us to get together,' he had broken out angrily. 'Are you trying to ruin my reputation?'

Clare had bit her lip to stop the smile which threatened. He had seen the amusement in her face, though, and he had looked even more furious.

'I won't be able to face them,' he had raved. 'They'll all laugh at me if they guess you've turned me down. It's in all the papers—they're waiting for us to start living together.'

'You shouldn't read your own publicity,' she advised sweetly.

She had felt sorry for him as she watched him. Under that handsome face and perfect physique was the mind of an adolescent. He was so used to women keeling over whenever he smiled at them that he didn't have a clue what to do in this situation.

'What am I going to say to them?' he demanded childishly.

'Try acting,' Clare smiled at him. 'It's time you learnt how to do some.'

He stalked off looking like Hamlet on the battlements of Elsinore, his eyes wounded.

Her career after that film had been meteoric. It had made her a big name, her face and figure instantly recognised wherever she went.

'Especially your figure,' Macey had teased. 'Who can blame them?'

Clare had learnt to take her looks seriously in a totally realistic sense. She knew how to present the image which the public expected of her. Her looks were part of her stock-in-trade and she looked after them. At twenty-seven she was cool, clear-headed and ambitious. She had made her name in films, but she still preferred the theatre because the adrenalin which surged into her veins came from a live audience. The two-way communication one got on a stage meant more to her than the money she could earn in a film.

'Although the money's nice,' she had admitted to Macey, and he had given her a sardonic, appreciative look from the top of her light golden head to her hand-sewn Italian shoes, taking in all the slender curves of her body in the expensive London-designed dress on the way down.

'And, of course, poverty becomes you,' he had drawled.

'Sarcasm!' she had laughed back at him.

Macey was her bridge to reality. He would not let her head be turned by all the public adulation she had received after her film. His cool, ironic eyes punctured an ego quicker than a pin stuck into a balloon.

She felt him moving restlessly beside her now. His own success had not made him invulnerable to the tension of each new attempt. The play she was reading was his latest. Clare was the first person to read it, and Macey was strung-up as he waited for her verdict. The central role was a part which she had slowly recognised as being based on herself. Macey had made no attempt to disguise the fact. His shrewd analysis of her character was no surprise to her. Macey's reading of

motivation and human nature was well known to her.
But one scene had struck her forcibly. The girl suddenly broke out into a poignant speech which showed
Clare that, although she had never confided in Macey,
he had somehow deduced something of what had happened to her to make her emotionally and physically
withdrawn.

Clare had read the scene three times now. She went
on to finish the play quite quickly before closing the
script and turning to look levelly at Macey.

He caught the mock-accusation in her green eyes
and flung up his hands in a wry gesture. 'Don't shoot!
I'm innocent.'

'And clever,' Clare murmured drily.

'Good guesswork?' Macey watched her, one dark
brow arching upwards, his mouth level.

'I'm not sure I like having my past disinterred in
public and the remains picked over by a literary rag-
and-bone man.'

'Sorry, ma'am,' Macey mocked softly.

'Especially when he's just guessing!'

'It makes good theatre, doesn't it?'

'So that's all I mean to you,' she retorted. 'Canni-
bal!'

The sideways flick of his blue eyes moved away
almost at once. 'I won't use it without your permission.
I don't need to tell you that, do I, Clare?'

She fingered the pages of the script, staring down
the terraced levels of the garden. The rocky coast below
them danced in a heat haze which softened the rugged
outlines where the land met the sea. Macey had rented

this house from a wealthy London businessman who kept it for annual holidays himself but, typically, liked to make even his pleasure pay for its keep. When Clare agreed to stay there she hadn't been aware that Macey was writing. Her first week had been spent just lying here in the sun or idly cruising around the large open-air swimming pool which lay to one side of the house. Macey had worked with dedicated concentration, only appearing at mealtimes or in the evenings.

There had been other guests that week, all of them theatre people, friends of both Clare and Macey. Conversation had been mutually limited to small talk about the weather or the scenery. They had all wanted to relax and do nothing very much. The others had left yesterday, brown as berries and reluctant to return to London after their days in the sun. Now Macey and Clare were alone in the villa.

That didn't bother her. She was too used to Macey's constant presence to be aware of him as anything but the friend and ally he had become over the years.

'Well?' Macey asked lightly, and she looked round at him.

'Will you do it?' he asked.

'Try and stop me.' Her sudden smile made his eyes gleam.

'You have impeccable taste—I've told you that before.'

She laughed. 'Flatterer!' She fluttered the pages of the script. 'First, you'll have to interest a management.'

'I already have,' he drawled in pretended indifference.

She sat up. 'Who?'

'Phil.' Macey stretched his long body in a yawn. 'We talked it over three months ago. I outlined the idea and he said he liked it. He wanted a new play for the spring.'

'He hasn't read it yet, though?'

'I wanted you to read it first. I couldn't have done it if you rejected the idea.'

'It's good,' she said gently. 'Far too good for me to stand in your light, Macey.'

He turned his dark head and sunlight glinted on his blue eyes, the strong line of cheek and jaw relaxed as he lay there. Macey had looks which were distinctly individual, the intelligence behind the blue eyes sharpening the impact of his features. His mouth was beautifully formed and powerful with a discipline which the fleshless structure of his face reinforced.

'Now that I've your promise to take the lead, nothing will stand in my light. Such a *big* star, darling!'

'I don't know why I put up with that tongue of yours,' Clare told him with amusement.

'You love me,' Macey murmured, his mouth twisting sardonically.

'Oh, is that it? It's news to me.'

She caught the blue flash of his eyes and heard him laugh under his breath. 'No wonder our famous friend said you were a frigid little bitch,' Macey drawled.

She had told him about her last encounter with the great heart-throb of the silver screen. She told Macey everything—everything except the one fact about her that made sense of everything else.

The telephone rang distantly in the house and with a deep groan Macey pulled himself out of the chair. 'That can't be anyone I want to talk to, but I suppose I'll have to answer it.'

She watched him walk away, his black shadow moving on the ground behind him in dancing mimicry. Even now there was the faintest resemblance in Macey to the man who had destroyed her emotional resources that night long ago. It was not in the features that that fleeting impression lay—it was merely in his colouring, his build. At a quick glance she could still feel her heart beat sickeningly when Macey moved, especially if she did not see his face.

Macey's play had brought it all back to her mind, not that it was ever far away. She had had it in the background of her head for nine long years, and she was unable to forget a second of that night.

She lay back in the lounger with the dark glasses shielding her eyes, and the sun pouring down over her relaxed body, listening to the far-off whisper of the sea on the rocky shore.

I must have a great capacity for love, she thought ironically. I'm a concentrated hater.

She had only met him once, so briefly, but if she closed her eyes she could always remember him.

All the men she had ever met had failed to get through the ice crystals which had formed on her that night. She lay in the sun, shivering, as though it were deepest winter. She had flown like Icarus too close to the heat of the sun and plunged, like him, the false wax melting, drowning in cold seas.

He was a myth to her now, something not quite real which had shaped her at a formative moment in her life, and in some ways, Clare thought wryly, she owed him a debt of gratitude because she had been so very young for her age; bemused and bewildered by London after a strangely innocent upbringing. If she hadn't met him that night, sooner or later she would have met someone else who would have attempted to use her in the same way, but with more lasting results. He had been a grim warning to her. She had learnt from that brief experience to keep men at a distance, refuse to let them blackmail, bribe, coax her. She had climbed in her profession by talent alone, rejecting all the quicker routes which her looks would have made so easy.

She was under no illusions about that. She had been offered such chances again and again. Clare knew that many girls with ambition accepted them, shrugging philosophically, but she had never noticed that it got them far. In the last resort, talent was all that mattered.

Clare had changed radically from that New Year party. The innocent wide-eyed girl had become a sophisticated woman of twenty-seven whose huge green eyes and sensuous body were plastered all over magazines and posters. Her hair had been styled in light, curling strands which blew around her head, making her look like a sexy boy until one saw the rounded body below her head.

The wind lifted them now and blew them restlessly and Macey dropped down beside her suddenly, brushing his hand across the windswept curls in a light caress.

'That was Rowena.'

'Rowena?' she queried.

'She's at Nice and wants us to drive over for dinner tonight.'

'You didn't accept?' Clare felt too heavily relaxed to sit around talking to people this evening. She did not want to stir. She had been working very hard during the past year and this was her first real break.

'People don't refuse Rowena's invitations.'

'I would have.'

Macey laughed drily. 'I can just hear you! You're scared stiff of her.'

'Who isn't?' Clare smiled at him, her eyes hidden behind the dark glasses. Rowena had a frozen stare when anyone attempted to treat her as anything but the very pinnacle of perfection. For forty years she had sat up there; a worshipped goddess, smiling benignly on her adoring audiences, her briefest utterances treated as divine writ. Clare would not seriously challenge Rowena's divinity.

'What time shall we have to leave?' she asked, sighing in resigned acceptance.

'Six-thirty,' Macey told her, his eyes amused. 'Which just gives you time to make yourself beautiful if you start now.' His wicked eyes mocked her.

'I'm too lazy to hit you, so shut up,' she told him, stretching herself with a graceful, supple movement which kept Macey's eyes pinned to her. Clare was not unaware of his stare, but she was too used to it to do more than register in passing that Macey was conscious of the sensuous lines of her figure. Macey was male, very much so, but Clare had no alarm when he watched her. Custom had made him safe for her.

'You've never worked with Rowena, have you?' Macey asked some time later, and she shook her head.

'Like to?'

The casual tone made her turn her head abruptly, staring at him sharply. She jumped at it in a flash, her eyes widening. 'You aren't hoping to interest her in the part of the vile old harridan in the boarding house?'

Macey assumed a bland smile. 'She could read it, I suppose.'

Clare whistled under her breath. 'You've got nerve, I'll say that for you!'

'Of course,' he said in self-satisfaction. 'I'm a genius.'

'And modest with it,' she said, starting to laugh. Surveying him with amusement, she added, 'Darling Macey, she wouldn't touch it with a bargepole.'

'We'll see,' said Macey.

'Who are you getting for the old man? Now, who's so famous that his name would drag them in off the streets if he was reading the telephone directory?'

'I want the best cast I can get.'

'So I see, you shrinking little violet. I'm honoured you came to me first.'

'So you should be,' he informed her with a wicked little smile which made his blue eyes as bright as the far-off sea. 'You're going to dazzle them in it.'

'Don't think I can't read you like a book. I shall expect a cut of the royalties—fifty per cent, I think. Having been so cleverly cannibalised I feel I deserve it.'

'You aren't annoyed?' His quick look was intent.

Clare studied him. 'Would it make any difference if I were?'

'You could sue.'

'So I could.' Clare closed her eyes, pushing her sunglasses back up her nose. 'I'll think about it.'

There was a long silence. The olive trees rustled busily in the sea breeze and a bee hummed happily as it raided the roses.

'How close was I, Clare?'

The quiet, level question made her tense, but she kept her eyes shut and her face did not give a thing away. 'Mmm?' she murmured in a drowsy voice.

'Was that how it happened?'

'What are we talking about?' she enquired, pretending to yawn.

'Something like that happened,' Macey went on coolly. 'When I met you, you were already locked up tight and you've stayed like it ever since. At first I just thought you were as cold as charity, but over the years I've come to know you too well to believe that any more. Someone, somewhere, hit you so hard you've never given anyone else a chance to get within a foot of you.'

'Thank you, Doctor Freud, and goodnight,' Clare drawled, flapping a lazy hand over her mouth in a mock yawn.

He laughed shortly. 'Okay, I'll drop the subject, but you're too lovely to waste your sweetness on the desert air, Clare. In all the years I've known you, you've never looked twice at anyone, but on stage you give out excitement like an electric storm. It has to be in there, waiting for the right man.' His voice deepened, grew husky. 'What are you looking for, Clare? Don't you know me well enough to give me a tiny clue?'

'I'm very fond of you, Macey,' Clare said, keeping her eyes shut and struggling to keep her voice cool, 'but if you don't shut up I'll take the first plane back to London.'

After that, he didn't say a single thing.

CHAPTER THREE

SHE slid back into a physical relaxation which did not match the tormented confusion of her thoughts. Macey and his damned play had brought it all back too vividly for her. She could still wince at the memory of her eighteen-year-old self walking blindly, blissfully into strange arms on a tide of romantic illusion which had ended, as all illusion ends, in tears and betrayal.

Luke had been so irresistibly attractive, the physical allure matched by a smiling charm, and she had been far too romantic; wide-eyed with the belief that love, true love, was waiting round a corner for her. She had not thought beyond each magic moment of that evening. While he was kissing her, she had been rapt on a tide of delight, never suspecting how far his intentions went because love, to her, had been a question of emotion rather than physical pleasure.

The bitter humiliation of waking up, sober, to realise

precisely how he saw her, in what role he had cast her, she had been carrying with her ever since. She had woken up on a cold hillside and she would never again wander into those treacherous realms of love.

Macey had, of course, only taken a stab at the truth, because he had had to use his imagination, and in the play the heroine's betrayal had come in very different circumstances, but it had come close enough to make her very wary of Macey. He saw too much and he was too clever.

She shook off her disturbed thoughts and got up. Macey blinked, looking up at her through half-lowered lids.

'I think I'll have a swim before I change for dinner,' she told him as she turned away.

'You do that,' he murmured lazily. 'I'll stay where I am, thank you, and watch. You're very watchable.'

She pretended to smile, but her mouth moved stiffly and she knew he observed the movement with intent scrutiny.

She walked towards the pool with him staring after her and sank into the artificially blue water. She did a rapid crawl from one end of the pool to the other before turning on to her back and idling along, her smooth golden skin gleaming wet under the afternoon sun.

A pity they had to drive to Nice, she thought. She was enjoying total idleness. The tensions and nervous irritations of work had faded from her mind during the last week. She had needed these days in the sun.

She clambered out of the pool and Macey stood up in a stretching, graceful movement. He stared at her as she walked back to him, her wet hair plastered to her head.

'You swim like a fish,' he observed, running his eyes down over her. 'But you're not shaped like one.'

'Deathless lines,' Clare mocked, walking towards the house.

'If I wrote words that burned the paper they were written on you'd only laugh,' he retorted drily.

'If you wrote words that burned the paper they were written on you'd be wasting your time, surely?'

'Don't I know it?' There was a sudden savage note in his voice which made her whole body tense. She glanced at him nervously over her shoulder, but when she saw his face he was smiling coolly.

They separated and Clare went to her bedroom to shower and wash the chlorine from her hair before blow-drying it into the feather-light golden waves which clung around her head to give her a sophisticated beauty her green eyes emphasised.

She sat on her dressing-table stool wrapped in a big lemon-yellow towel, brushing her drying hair as she turned the hair-dryer from one side to the other. She didn't hear the little knock above the sound of the machine, but when the door opened and Macey peered round it she glanced sideways at him in surprise.

'I knocked,' he said, smiling. 'I forgot to warn you—Rowena will be wearing blue, she informed me, so whatever you do stay away from the colour blue.'

Clare's eyes danced. 'I'm tempted.'

'Don't be,' he said drily. 'She'd never forget it.'

She nodded, shrugging. 'Okay.'

Turning back to the mirror, she went on with her hair, but Macey didn't go. She could hear him standing there, his body motionless but his muted breathing oddly audible. Sliding a glance at him, she met his eyes with an inward tremor. Macey gave her a dry smile and went out, closing the door.

Clare was dismayed to find her face very flushed when she looked back at it. Macey had been staring at her so strangely, the set of his mouth hard, his eyes narrowed.

She told herself she was imagining it. Macey had shown signs of attraction to her in the past, but that was all long ago. He hadn't made a single pass for years.

Although Rowena was in her sixties she remained a challenge which no self-respecting actress would refuse. Clare took great trouble in dressing for the evening. Rowena was famous for her snubbing sharpness in certain moods. People bore with her because they had no choice. Genius makes its own rules, and nobody imagined Rowena was not a genius. Clare admired her, revered her and was terrified of her. Those cold, marble blue eyes could annihilate with a look. Rowena's wit could be deadly, and Clare had no intention of becoming a target for Rowena's amusement.

Macey eyed her when she joined him with a lifted brow. 'Full armour, darling?'

'Absolutely. I know Rowena,' she nodded.

'Not yet you don't,' Macey informed her. 'You may think you do. I think one reason why Rowena's invited us over is to get a closer look at you. Rowena always sizes up the opposition.'

'Me? I'm no threat to her.'

'Every actress under sixty is a threat to Rowena.'

'Well, I suppose that does cover me, just about,' she smiled.

'I'm not joking, Clare. Keep your shield up while we're there.'

'What do you think this is?' she demanded, turning on one toe in a little pirouette.

'Full battle order, from the look of you,' Macey agreed, his eyes running slowly from the bright sleek head, over the smooth golden shoulders exposed by her green dress, down the curved line of breast, waist and thigh to the long silken legs. 'You're quite something when you're dressed to kill.'

'I admire Rowena, but she isn't treating me like a walk-on in a Christmas panto. I've seen her do it— and to ladies who should have been able to hold their own. Not me, though, Macey—Rowena isn't flattening me!'

'If I were a wiser man I'd stay at home and watch the telly,' Macey drawled.

'No, you wouldn't, because blood and thunder is your staple diet.'

'So long as it isn't a massacre,' said Macey, sounding dry, as he guided her out of the house.

'Which of us do you think is for the chop? Or can I guess?'

Macey eyed her sideways as he started the car. 'Darling, you're clever and witty, but Rowena's been eating people for breakfast since before you were born.'

'Time she stopped, then. She'll get indigestion.'

'Not Rowena. She has a cast-iron digestion.'

Clare laughed. 'Are you trying to frighten me?'

'Just a word of gentle warning. I love you and I don't want to see Rowena getting her teeth into you.'

They turned towards Nice at a steady pace, the car purring. The town lay sprawled in the evening sunshine, the houses falling down steep hills in terraces, the white walls and red roofs picturesque, given a hint of tropical somnolence by palm trees whose shadows etched the deepening sky.

Macey shot her another look. 'Darling, when you've been on a stage with Rowena you'll know why it's best to go on your knees rather than quarrel with her. She can ruin a performance without you even knowing she's doing it. The audience don't even know what's going on! She'll fidget with her hair or straighten her dress, and every man jack in the place is watching her, because Rowena makes people watch her. On a stage she's a magnet. Even sitting absolutely still she can somehow make people watch her. If she decides to she can destroy anyone acting with her. So watch it, Clare. Don't antagonise her.'

She smiled. 'All right, Machiavelli.'

Macey drove, both hands moving on the steering wheel as they took the terrifying bends of the mountain road, on one side the sheer hillside, on the other a plunge into empty space which made Clare's eye stay riveted on Macey rather than look the other way.

When they arrived at Rowena's villa they were ushered into a long, lemon-walled room which seemed full of people. After a moment Clare sorted out the apparent crowd scene into three people and Rowena— Rowena was a crowd scene all by herself.

She was dressed in a high-necked, long-sleeved blue dress which somehow managed to make her taller and more striking than ever. About a hundred thin gold chains hung clinking round her neck; Clare could imagine what damage they would do to anyone acting on a stage with Rowena. An audience wouldn't hear a word. Rowena swept forward, accompanied by a silvery metallic sound like tiny bells. Although she was in her sixties she looked so much younger that Clare could scarcely believe her eyes. Rowena moved like a young girl, the faint wrinkling of her long throat veiled by that clever, concealing neckline. Her skin had a smoothness which Clare suspected owed much to brilliant make-up technique. Her blue eyes were enormous, very bright and very watchful.

Clare watched her touch a cheek warily to Macey's face. 'Darling Macey, how lovely to see you! You are good to spare some of your precious time to come and see me.'

'I dropped everything and ran,' said Macey, his smile coaxing.

'Flatterer,' said Rowena, not displeased.

Macey took her hand and bowed over it in an elegant movement, his lips brushing the back. 'It's very good of you to invite us—we were thrilled.'

Rowena graciously turned towards Clare, her smile painted on her mouth but not continuing in her blue eyes. Clare felt the piercing shaft of those eyes as they ran over her.

'How lovely you look, my dear,' Rowena said in her beautiful voice with extreme coldness.

Clare gave her a wide-eyed, awed look. It wasn't all acting. She was finding it a considerable shock to stand here, facing a woman whose acting she had always admired to the point of adoration. She had met Rowena several times before, but never felt those blue eyes actually looking at her. Rowena only noticed people she felt deserved to be noticed, and until now Clare hadn't come within the range of Rowena's Olympian vision.

Now the piercing blue eyes pinned her down and she did not need to pretend to be awestruck. She *was* awestruck.

Rowena, at close quarters, was quite terrifying.

'I saw you in *The Wild Duck*,' Rowena intoned in that voice which could ring in the mind like a drowned bell. 'Poignant performance. I was quite well received in that part myself a few years back.'

A good forty years back, Clare thought, remembering the date of Rowena's famous appearance in the part.

Aloud she said, 'That's the great difficulty of the classics. One is always aware of the great performances of the past and always afraid one can never match them.'

'You can only try, my dear,' said Rowena, so sweetly that Clare smiled, although she was very conscious of the hidden thrust beneath the words.

'And what are you doing at the moment?' Rowena asked with apparent interest.

Clare gazed at her innocently. 'I'm between parts, I'm afraid.'

Rowena's smile was a miracle of benevolence. 'They'll come, my dear, they'll come.' She turned, waving a graceful hand. 'Now, have you met my husband?'

Clare shook hands with Ted Kilby, exchanging brief smiles with him. He was a painter who spent most of his time in the south of France, as she knew from Macey. Faintly balding, short and sturdy, with spatulate hands and a dry way of talking, he took little part in Rowena's public life. They had, however, been married for more than thirty years and were apparently ideally suited. Rowena had little room for a private life, anyway, and Ted Kilby's remote personality suited her own.

'And this is my business manager,' Rowena went on, her hand under Clare's elbow. 'Bob Ryland.'

He was a man of around forty, his manner smooth as silk, his clothes expensive, his smile over-polite. Clare didn't much care for him. She found the roaming assessment of his dark eyes offensive.

'And you know Ray, of course,' Rowena said.

Clare turned without any particular delight. 'Hallo, Ray.'

'Hallo,' said Ray Gordon, her dark eyes cold. Ray had been in love with Macey for some time; Macey either did not know or preferred not to admit he had noticed. Clare realised that Ray's hostility towards her was born of jealousy, but could hardly go out of her way to tell her that the jealousy was misplaced. If she had thought Macey returned Ray's feelings she might have done something to clear Ray's mind but, since Macey showed no sign of doing that, Clare let it go.

Tall, languid, with cloudy black hair and a beautiful pale skin, Ray was an actress of considerable talent. She was also Rowena's niece. Clare had forgotten that. Rowena had no children of her own and had always publicly made much of Ray, proud of her talent and not above giving her a helping hand if she thought it necessary.

Ray would, in any case, have made it on her own. Clare had seen her give some intelligent and beautiful performances.

'What will you have to drink?' Bob Ryland asked at Clare's elbow.

'A dry Martini, thank you,' she said, giving him a brief smile.

'You're staying at Macey's villa?' Ray asked in a stilted little voice, her eyes lowered.

'Yes.'

'Graham and Liz are there, too, aren't they?' Ray murmured. 'You should have brought them.'

'They left yesterday,' said Clare, and Ray's dark lashes flickered before lifting. Her dark eyes shot towards Macey who met her glance blankly.

He turned to take his glass from Bob Ryland's hand, and Ray stared at his averted profile with a deeply intent look that made Clare feel strangely sick. Oh, God, she thought. Poor Ray. How can she bear to go on feeling like that about a man who just ignores her?

Ray was so beautiful and the way she felt was so unhidden. Did she make any attempt to hide it? Didn't she care that everyone who saw her with Macey could tell how she felt?

In a long, cloudy glass behind Ray's head she caught sight of Macey. His brown skin gleamed, his intelligent blue eyes were veiled by his lids. There was no expression in his face at all, he looked as though he were asleep, yet she knew that that look betrayed Macey's hidden thoughts. When he was deep in observation he looked like that. His brain was clicking away behind those hidden eyes.

He turned his head and in the mirror their eyes met. Macey didn't smile. He just looked at her and it was Clare who looked away, a shiver running down her spine.

At times she felt almost frightened of Macey. She felt like that now. The cold, impassive man whose eyes had just met her own in the cloudy glass had been strangely alarming. Macey's warmth and vitality were only shadows of what went on behind his mask of a face. The mind which had spawned his clever, startling plays was remote from that face and Clare guessed she knew little of what went on inside that mind.

Rowena watched Clare accept her Martini from Bob Ryland. 'We're hoping for another arrival,' she told her almost coyly. 'Keep your fingers crossed that his plane was on time.'

Clare looked at her enquiringly, smiling.

'My wife's godson,' Ted Kilby explained. 'He was due in from the States this evening and Rowena is hoping to have him here for dinner if he's recovered from jet-lag.'

There was a ring at the door a moment later and Rowena gave a little cry of delight. 'He's here, he's here!'

It was as much a performance as her usual behaviour. Rowena had probably never acted spontaneously in her life. Her smile was wide and genuine, however, and she moved to the door as it opened with her hands outstretched and a welcome bubbling to her lips.

Clare glanced idly across the room and all the colour seeped out of her face as she suddenly recognised the man greeting Rowena.

Her hand began to shake. The pale liquid in her glass spilled and Macey turned to look at her sharply. Clare struggled to pull herself together, dragging on the broken reins of her self-assurance, fighting down a desire to run out of the room. She heard Rowena excitedly talking yet could not take in a word. She stood there, staring at the newcomer, and shook so much she had to put down her glass.

Her eyes shot away and met Macey's fixed, narrow stare. She felt her colour come back with a terrible rush and looked down.

He hadn't altered. Or very little. Perhaps there were fine threads of silver in the black hair. His features were more arrogant than she remembered, carried a little more self-satisfaction. She was seeing him now with eyes that saw clearly, far more clearly than they had on that first occasion. She could now read the self-willed sensuality in the line of his mouth, the cruelty in the grey eyes.

She looked up and took in his face again. Her sight

was beginning to clear from the peculiar hazed mist which had seemed to obscure it when she first recognised him, and she felt very cold, her skin prickling. He was talking to Ray now, holding her hand and looking down at her with the deliberate charm Clare recognised only too painfully. Ray talked lightly, smiling. They obviously knew each other very well. Rowena was watching them indulgently.

Clare's hand groped for her glass again. She lifted it to her mouth and drained the contents. It might help. She had to get through this moment somehow. Surely she could act well enough to disguise her shock?

Macey had already noticed it. She guessed that from the way he was watching her now, his stare intent and searching. But it wasn't Macey's observation that was bothering her. An icy sensation was sweeping over her as she contemplated how Luke would look at her in a moment.

He hadn't seen her yet. He hadn't even glanced her way. What would his face reveal when he did? Her teeth clenched at the thought of him lifting one of those black eyebrows, smiling, his grey eyes reminding her of their night together.

She was so tense her hands were sweating. If she had had the nerve she would have got herself another drink, but she wasn't going to do anything which might draw attention to her. She had to stand there like a fool, shivering, sick with shame and self-loathing.

Even after nine years the memory of her own humiliation was so strong that all her self-possession had deserted her.

Rowena extended an embracing arm, saying, 'Macey darling, this is my godson, Luke Murry. Luke, this is one of our brightest new talents—Macey Janson.'

Macey was shaking hands, his voice very cool, his face wearing a smile which did not reach his eyes. Clare picked up the sensations inside Macey and realised that he did not like Luke. Macey did not often take a dislike to people, but he had taken one to Luke Murry.

'That last play of yours was terrific,' Luke told him. 'I was fascinated. When I read it in print it seemed quite different. On stage it had a peculiar menace one couldn't quite pin down.'

'Oh?' Macey asked with offhand indifference.

Luke looked at him and smiled again. Clare watched the charm she remembered and saw that it could not touch Macey, whose face stayed hard. 'That second act was quite spine-chilling.'

'Kind of you to say so,' Macey told him tersely.

'Luke's a businessman, but he's very interested in the theatre,' Rowena told Macey, looking at him in surprise as she recognised that Macey was being difficult.

'My firm makes steel components,' Luke said.

'How fascinating,' Macey drawled icily.

Rowena gave a high, slightly artificial peal of laughter. 'Don't be naughty, Macey.' Her offended glance warned him to be more pleasant and when his face stayed immovable she glanced at Clare. 'I'd forgotten you, my dear. Luke, this is Clare Barry.'

Clare slowly, tensely moved forward, her stomach churning with fear and shock. Luke Murry's grey eyes moved over her smilingly. He held out his hand and

as she tremblingly put her own into his grasp one
thought ran round and round her head.

He didn't remember her.

'I recognised you, of course,' he said, still holding
her hand. The grey eyes glinted in a mockery she remembered clearly. 'New York was covered with posters
of you last year. One couldn't drive a block without
seeing that beautiful face.'

She somehow found the strength to pretend light
laughter. 'What a shame!'

'Oh, I missed them when they came down,' he told
her, one brow flickering. 'You brightened the mornings
for me.'

'How nice,' she said, fluttering her lashes at him and
deftly detaching her hand from his possession. Her
mind was dissolving in sensations of sheer loathing. She
had to fight a desire to rub her hand against her dress
to remove all taint of his fingers. He didn't recognise
her at all, except as the star of that film. She could
scarcely believe it. The grey eyes held nothing but
charming flattery, the accustomed sexual invitation of
a man who likes women and is usually liked by them.

'What was it like shooting the film out in the desert?
Not very comfortable, I imagine.' He watched her as
he asked, smiling.

'Not very,' Clare agreed. She lifted her bright golden
head and gave him the benefit of her most brilliant,
most artificial smile. 'Sand in everything you ate, like a
picnic on the beach. Flies everywhere. Make-up running, and people always in a temper because it was so
hot. I was always thirsty and always feeling grubby. I

wouldn't want to work in those conditions again.'

She was talking in a light, brittle voice which sounded as if it might snap at any moment. Macey was staring fixedly at her, and she carefully kept her eyes averted from him because Macey was too quick, too clever, too dangerous. She wasn't sure what he had already noticed, but she knew he had noticed something. She did not want him to get too much information from her face. Her eyes would give her away if Macey got the chance to see them.

'It was a good film,' said Luke Murry. She had her eyes on his mouth, forcing down sickness because the movements of his warm, hard lips reminded her too vividly of the feel of them against her own, the incredible and destructive effect they had had on her that night.

She had been kissed since, not very often in private, and never with any pleasure. Looking at his mouth as he spoke she hurriedly looked away, because her pulses were pounding stormily and she couldn't bear to remember how it had felt.

He didn't even remember, she reminded herself.

For nine years he had scarred her life, and he had forgotten it ever happened. She had been one of a long procession passing through his bed; a cheap little conquest picked up at a party who hadn't been as easy as he had expected. He probably hadn't even remembered who he had taken to bed that night. When he woke up in the morning alone, perhaps he hadn't spared a thought for what had happened the night before. She had been less than nothing to him, yet he had been the formative experience of her whole life.

There was a peculiar silence.

She looked up, her skin flushing. Everyone was staring at her. Glancing into Luke Murry's eyes she saw amusement and cynical irritation in them, and belatedly she realised that he had asked her a question and was waiting for an answer.

Macey answered for her, his voice light and cool. 'She said he would eat garlic before their big love scenes.'

Everyone laughed. Luke Murry still watched her, his mouth hard. He wasn't used to having women's attention wander while he was talking to them. He didn't like it.

'You didn't tell him that? Good heavens, his ego will never recover!' Ray spoke brightly and Luke turned to look at her, his black brows flickering in a movement Clare remembered.

She remembered everything, she realised. There wasn't a single thing about him she had not absorbed and retained.

She had known Macey so well for so long, yet in one night Luke Murry had stamped his image so profoundly on her memory that even the fleeting expressions of his face seemed more deeply familiar to her than anything about Macey.

She looked away and found herself facing Macey at that moment. She wished she hadn't looked in his direction. His eyes were hard and probing and he was frowning slightly. His mouth was straight and cold, a hard line which did not soften as he stared at her.

He moved closer to her and in an instinctive attempt to distract him she ran her hand through his arm, hoping he would not be able to feel how it trembled or how cold her skin was, giving him a quick, upwards smile as she leaned against him.

Macey did not smile back, but his arm closed on her hand, pressing it against him. He glanced down and at this angle she saw a hardness in the line of jaw and cheekbone. His blue eyes had a harsh light she had never seen in them before. They were unfamiliar to her. She did not know them. Staring at him, she could not imagine why she had ever thought she saw anything of Luke Murry in Macey. There wasn't even the slightest resemblance. Macey would never be handsome. His face was strong and compelling rather than handsome; there was no shadow of sensuality in it.

She knew Macey was trying to work out exactly why she had reacted like that to the sight of Luke Murry. He had watched with fixed intensity as she shook hands with the other man and he must have realised that Luke, at least, had shown no sign of recognition. Macey was puzzled and he wouldn't give up until he knew what had made her go white and tremble at the sight of Luke.

She swallowed, looking away. She couldn't bear to have Macey know. He must not find out. She had to act like mad to make him think he had imagined it all.

Someone moved towards them and Macey looked at the newcomer with a warm smile. 'Hallo, Kate. How are you?'

Clare glanced towards the other woman in surprise

and Macey looked down at her again. 'You haven't met Kate, have you? She's Rowena's secretary. Kate, this is Clare Barry.'

Kate offered her hand, her pale eyes pleasant. She was a woman in her early forties; thin, rather self-effacing in dress yet with clear intelligence in her eyes and the faintest gleam of a humour not openly expressed.

'Kate's been with Rowena for years,' Macey told her.

'Remarkable stamina,' commented Clare, meeting Kate's eyes with a quick smile.

Macey threw a glance over his shoulder, but Rowena was talking loudly with graceful gestures while the others in the room stood around her laughing. Clare's remark had not been heard.

'She's a phenomenon,' Kate said with an amused little smile, shaking her head. 'I love working for her. I could earn more and have a much easier life working for some vast organisation, but even in her toughest moods Rowena is still a genius, and I wouldn't have missed a day of it.'

'I can imagine,' said Clare. 'I'd still require danger money if I worked for her.'

'For God's sake, Clare!' Macey muttered.

She was in a reckless mood. She laughed at him, her green eyes bright and dancing. 'She won't hear me.'

They all paused, listening as the bell-like voice rang out behind them. Everyone around Rowena laughed obediently as she paused. Clare picked out another famous name from what Rowena said next, and wondered what that eminent actress would say if she could hear what Rowena was saying about her. Outrage would have been a mild reaction, she thought, suppressing a smile. Rowena was not sparing her.

'He had put vodka in the lemonade,' Rowena said piercingly, 'and by the third act she was barely able to walk—not that it made much difference. Drunk or sober, she couldn't act her way out of a paper bag.'

Kate met Clare's eyes. 'Totally untrue, of course, but funny.' She looked at Macey. 'Have you brought your play with you?'

He grinned at her. 'Of course. I won't ask how she's viewing the idea.'

'I wouldn't tell you if you did!'

'I'm aware of that,' he returned, mocking her.

'Or he'd ask,' Clare said sweetly.

Macey gave her a threatening look and Kate laughed.

'And I'm aware of that! I'm used to dealing with unscrupulous egotists.'

'That puts you in your place,' Clare informed Macey, her smile teasing.

Kate moved away, smiling, and Macey looked into Clare's green eyes with a twisted little smile. 'One day I'll put you in your place,' he muttered before turning away.

She laughed, but a second later wondered exactly what he had meant. She had a feeling that that had been one of Macey's two-edged lines.

The dinner table was dominated by Rowena's regal presence. She held them all, talking in her beautiful, sonorous voice and refusing to let anyone stray from the circle of her audience. Clare discovered that when the barbed thrust of her cruel wit came, it was delivered in a beautifully modulated voice which somehow sharpened the cut of the blow. Rowena used her voice as a weapon and it was fatally effective.

Macey listened and laughed and looked as though the only thought in his head was of Rowena. Clare knew it wasn't the case. She could feel his attention even when he wasn't looking at her. Macey sent out thought waves and Clare received them loud and clear.

He was curious, alert, busy putting two and two together and making God knew what. Quick, clever, dangerous Macey, Clare thought, drinking her wine with her eyes bent on her plate. She was going to have to guard her tongue. He could see through brick walls. She didn't want him so much as guessing at the truth.

Macey had said to her once: 'It's the context that matters.' He had been talking about one of his ambiguous lines. Clare had complained that she didn't follow it. 'What does it mean?' she had demanded, and Macey had told her it was not so much what was said as how and why.

That was how Clare felt about the night she had spent with Luke Murry. It was not so much what he had done to her, but how and why. If some genuine emotion had driven him, the searing brand would never have burnt her spirit. He had treated her like a little tramp, and she had behaved like one. It didn't help to remind herself that she had been very young and very innocent, that she wasn't accustomed to drink and that she had been alone in a vast city which she found strange and disorientating.

She couldn't shrug off what had happened. He had given her an image of herself which had horrified, scarred, disgusted her.

She had determined never to let such a thing happen to her again. Whatever the cost in emotional emptiness, she had determined never to let a man get too close to her again. She wasn't ending up like the sad flotsam of her profession, drifting with the tide, sinking to the cold and lonely depths without a hand lifted to save them.

Ever since that night, the very idea of a man touching her had made her shudder in sick rejection.

Eating the bland lemon mousse which ended the meal, she decided she was relieved Luke Murry didn't remember her. It might make her humiliation worse, but at least he would never be able to tell anyone. She wouldn't have to endure the knowledge that Luke Murry could look at her and remember her in his arms that night.

Her lashes lowered, she flicked a glance along the table to where he sat and found him watching her. She felt a cold shiver as she met the hard glint of the grey eyes.

He didn't remember, did he?

He wasn't an actor. He surely couldn't have been clever enough to disguise recognition in the split second between when their eyes met and when he spoke so casually and politely?

The very thought that Luke Murry did remember and was hiding it made her feel so ill she could barely bring herself to drink the strong coffee which arrived a moment later.

After dinner they all sat around talking while Ray took a seat at the piano and played some pieces of light operetta, gay waltz tunes to which her soft touch gave a muted nostalgia.

Rowena tackled Macey about the new play. Playful, slightly coy, she shook her head over the very idea that she should play such a part. 'Do you see me in it? Do you really, Macey?'

'She's pathetic,' said Macey, wheedling her silkily, his smile a miracle of flattery. 'A broken, wicked old thing, but you would have the audience in tears by the end of the play.'

'She sounds appalling,' said Rowena, not displeased by the idea of making an audience weep. 'A strident old hag. Is that how you see me? I'm not noted for being strident, am I? I won't dispute that I'm an old hag.' Her laughter indicated that she did not believe a word of what she was saying.

'You can become anything you want to become,' Macey told her, smiling at her with the deep warmth which drew people to him whenever they saw him. 'Nobody would ever try to typecast you, Rowena.'

Rowena liked that. 'You think I could do it?' She moved her hands in a fluttering, silly way, her face suddenly stupid and vulgar yet pathetic, all her cold intelligence submerging. 'You think I could do the part? I don't know. I really don't know.'

'You're stupendous,' said Macey, laughing. 'That's exactly how I see her. You see, you don't even need make-up. You're a chameleon.'

It all fell away, dropping off like a discarded snakeskin, and Clare knew she had seen the first tentative groundwork of a performance. Rowena gave Macey a pleased little grin, oddly childlike and conspiratorial.

'I don't like long runs, though, my dear. Too tiring at my age. That's why I prefer revivals. I already know the words and they don't run too long. Three months is the most I can stand.'

'You'll be doing something new,' Macey agreed. 'I realise it will be a risk for you. I can understand it if you feel you don't want to work yourself to death, stretch yourself to the point of exhaustion.'

Rowena eyed him admiringly. 'Oh, you're quite frightening! Too clever. The right words every time. How can I resist a challenge like that?' She looked at her husband. 'What do you think, Ted? I'm tempted, I think I'm tempted.'

'You'll do it if you want to,' Ted Kilby said wryly. 'Don't pretend to ask my opinion. You know you never listen to a word I say.'

'I listen to what everybody says,' said Rowena, her hand sketching a circle and her eyes smiling at them all.

'And then you do just exactly what you want to do,' Ted finished for her.

Rowena gave him a long look, then turned to Macey. 'I'll read it. I can't say fairer than that, can I, Macey?'

'That's all I ask,' Macey said blandly.

They regarded each other with smiling, distrustful faces. 'Oh, yes,' Rowena said softly. 'You're clever and I don't trust you an inch.'

Rising to her feet, she crossed to the piano. 'Shall we have some Léhar? That won't bore everybody?' She didn't wait to be answered, flicking over the music on the piano.

Macey patted the seat next to him and Clare went over to sit beside him. 'She's biting,' he whispered, his eyes amused.

'And she's right about you,' Clare returned. 'You are clever and you can't be trusted an inch.'

Macey's eyes shot to her face. 'I know what Rowena's afraid of,' he drawled. 'But what's scaring you, Clare?'

She looked away, flushing, and saw the gleaming toecaps of Luke Murry's black shoes close behind them. He was standing with a glass in his hand and he was watching her and Macey. Clare felt a shiver run down her spine.

It was hard to believe that she was actually sitting here in a room with him, breathing the same air, without showing a sign of the sickness which rose in her throat every time she glanced in his direction.

Rowena was singing a cleverly fudged little song, blurring the notes because she couldn't hold them any more, yet with such clever technique that one was left with the impression that she could still sing. Ray's playing helped her, covering her lapses, rising to hide them. They had obviously worked out a routine.

Everyone clapped and Rowena gave them that satisfied little smile which made her somehow lovable. She had the childlike vanity of the very old combined with the love of applause which a life on the stage had given her.

'Macey, have you brought your play with you?' she asked a few moments later.

He nodded. 'It's in the car.'

'Get it, get it. I can't wait to read it. I shall read it in bed before I go to sleep. I always go to bed at eleven and it's five to now.'

Macey and Rowena went out to fetch the play. Clare watched Ted Kilby join Ray at the piano and suddenly began to feel nervous. She looked round to find Kate, and as she did so, Luke Murry sat down beside her, stretching his long legs with a lazy sigh.

'I wondered when I was going to get the chance,' he said, his eyes smiling down into her own.

Clare couldn't answer; her throat was too hot. She managed to lift her eyebrows in pretended surprise and Luke Murry laughed.

'Don't pretend you didn't know I've been trying to get you to myself all evening!'

The alarm she felt had become a nervous tension which was making her skin chill.

She was on a rack of doubt. Did he remember? Was he playing a game, a cat-and-mouse game which would end when he tired of it?

'Janson will be back in a minute,' he murmured. 'We must be quick. Have lunch with me tomorrow.'

Clare threw him a searching look. His face told her nothing. He was smiling at her, his grey eyes revealing no hint which could confirm or deny what she dreaded.

'I'm afraid——' she began, and he broke in on her stammered excuse with a smile which curled his lips and gave his handsome face that wry familiar mockery.

'Don't say no. I insist.'

For a moment her heart thudded too harshly for her

to answer. She stared, seeing that charm displayed for her again, the laughter lines at the corners of eye and mouth, the sensual smiling amusement.

Ted Kilby was playing ragtime, his strong wide hands deft and rhythmic, the heavy beat thudding beneath the melody.

Luke Murry turned to look at him. 'I love ragtime,' he said, giving Clare a sideways smile. 'Don't you?'

She didn't answer.

'Ted, play the Charleston,' Luke Murry said. He got a grin from Ted and then the music passed into that horribly familiar tune. Luke turned his dark head and looked into Clare's wide, stricken green eyes. 'Very nostalgic, isn't it?' he asked softly.

Her stomach was churning. He remembered.

'Lunch tomorrow? I'll pick you up at noon,' he said.

Macey came back into the room with Rowena, and Clare felt his eyes flick at once towards her and Luke Murry. Rowena was saying goodnight to everyone. She gave Clare a brief smile. 'Lovely of you to come,' she said before drifting out.

Clare stood up, fighting to control her face. Luke Murry rose with her, but she did not look at him again.

She smiled round the room, murmuring a farewell. Macey's hand took her elbow. His fingers hurt. Clare was almost glad of that; the needle-like pain helped her to shake free of the misery engulfing her. She walked out into the night with him, wishing she had not accepted Rowena's invitation. If she hadn't been there tonight she would never have met Luke Murry again.

CHAPTER FOUR

DRIVING home, Macey glanced at her and asked quietly: 'Okay, like to tell me?'

'Tell you what?' She raised her head with a defensive start and looked at him in wary questioning.

His mouth tightened. 'Don't fence.'

'What are you talking about?'

'The moment he walked in, you went white,' Macey said.

She curled her hands together in her lap and he shot his eyes down sideways to look at them. Clare hurriedly uncurled them, but Macey's glance came back to her face with dry emphasis.

'You're imagining things,' she lied huskily, trying to smile at him and only managing a pale imitation which did not convince him.

'Like hell!' Macey put his foot down and the car shot forward with a fierce roar. Clare glanced down the steep sides of the narrow, bending road, shuddering.

'Don't go so fast!'

His hands tightened on the wheel and he dropped the speed, staring ahead with an unsmiling face, the moonlight flickering over his features and leaving them taut and strange. 'He didn't bat an eyelid,' he said quietly. 'He's good. If I hadn't known you so well, I'd never have noticed a thing.'

Clare shivered. He was right: Luke Murry was good—as deceptive as a coiled cobra masquerading as part of the desert sands only to rear up and strike like a whiplash. He had had her fooled all evening; hoping, believing he had forgotten her, lulled into deceptive ease. He had been playing with her, amusing himself. Oh, God, I hate him, she thought in sick misery. What am I going to do?

She tried to pull her remnants of self-respect and brains together. What could Luke Murry do to harm her? Okay, he knew, he remembered. He wasn't going to go around boasting, for heaven's sake, and if he did, so what? This wasn't the Victorian age. Who would care?

I would, she thought, shivering. I'd care like hell. I don't want people knowing, staring, smiling.

And most of all, I don't want him knowing, staring, smiling. That was what she hated—the thought of being written down in Luke Murry's memory as an easy conquest, a cheap little tramp.

That was unbearable.

'Tell me,' Macey said huskily, and she looked round to find him watching her intently.

'There's no mystery,' she said in pretended lightness.

'Isn't there? I trust my instincts,' said Macey. 'And they picked up something from the moment he walked into the room.'

'Don't harp, Macey,' she said irritably.

He shrugged, frowning. 'If you won't tell me, you won't. But if you do ever decide you need a friendly ear, don't forget me.'

He couldn't possibly guess. His play had been an emotional stab at the truth, but the sordid nature of it hadn't entered his head. Macey was the last person in the world she could tell—she didn't want him knowing what had happened that night. He would look at her quite differently; she knew that. Macey had an image of her, and she didn't want that image shattered.

She looked at the sky and saw the moon hanging over the sea below them, wreathed in pale white mist, looking like a battered silver plate, the indentations and markings a grey blur of lines. The mysterious dark arms of palms wafted to and fro in the faint sea breeze. Somewhere a dog howled. Lights were going out in the little houses and villas, but along the coastal strip they stayed bright and constant, the hotels lit from roof to ground.

'Well, at least Rowena is biting,' Macey said drily. 'I can ring Phil and tell him the play has two possible stars.'

'One,' Clare corrected.

'What?' He slowed, staring at her. 'You aren't pulling out?'

'No, but with Rowena up front, there's only going to be one star,' Clare said with a smile.

He relaxed. 'I thought for one horrible moment that you were going to tell me you were changing your mind.'

'Why on earth should I?'

He threw her a piercing look. 'I don't know. I wish I did.'

She avoided his gaze. 'Well, you're stuck with me,' she said.

'I've known that for a long time,' said Macey, and Clare was surprised and taken aback, although his tone was wry and unemphatic.

They reached the villa a moment later and Macey garaged the car while Clare went inside and went at once to bed. Macey's last remark went on repeating inside her head. What had he meant? She stripped and showered, turning with closed eyes, trying to think and feeling so tired she couldn't manage to concentrate for long enough to get one coherent idea through her head.

It took her some time to get to sleep, and when she did sleep it was to dream and wake up sweating, crying out. The room was filled with perilous moonlight and a dark shape which moved as she sat up looking towards it.

She choked out a scream and the shape came over to the bed and she saw Macey's frowning face in the pale, mysterious light.

'Darling, what on earth is it? You've been screaming blue murder.'

Trembling, ice-cold, she leaned her face on his shoulder. He wasn't wearing a pyjama jacket and his body was warm. She laid her cheek on his skin, shivering.

'I'm sorry I woke you,' she whispered.

His hand stroked her tumbled hair, his arm around her tightly. 'Clare, tell me,' he whispered, and it was an entreaty; gentle, pleading.

She almost did and then couldn't, shaking her head.

'I must have eaten too much, or maybe that shellfish cocktail was off at dinner tonight.'

Macey's hands lifted her face and framed it while he stared at her. 'If you say so,' he said curtly.

She couldn't meet his eyes. 'I'm sorry I woke you. It must have been a shock to hear me yelling my head off.'

'I wasn't asleep.' She couldn't see his face. The moonlight touched his hair to silver, but his features were hidden.

'Oh,' she said, looking down, suddenly realising that neither of them was more than half-naked and that Macey's hand was moving up and down her spine in a convulsive way which made her grow tense.

'I expect I shall sleep better now,' she said shakily, not quite knowing how to move away from him.

Macey was breathing quickly, the sound raw and hoarse. 'Clare,' he muttered. His hand propelled her closer and his head came down. Many times in the past he had kissed her, lightly, gently, so that Clare had grown accustomed to the touch of his lips.

It was different this time. Before his mouth captured hers, she knew it would be different. Macey's tension had communicated itself to her own senses and the searching, hungry touch of his mouth reinforced what her intuition had told her.

She had a moment to think, to reject or accept, as he began to try to open her lips to his exploration.

Had he kissed her like that in the past she would have pushed him away in shocked surprise, but tonight she had been shaken to her roots by seeing Luke again. Closing her eyes, she blindly clung to Macey and her mouth parted. He gave a stifled moan and kissed her deeply, his arms tight around her.

It was comfort, security, a shared human contact which Clare felt she needed at that instant, and then it was something else, so suddenly that she was broken out of her compliant mood and made painfully aware that something had been unleashed in Macey which alarmed her.

He was breathing with a rough, irregular sound, his hand sliding over her bare shoulders, shaping her flesh, his fingertips tracing the hollow along her collarbone, pushing down the thin ribbon straps from which her nightgown fell, and the warm tenderness of his mouth had become hard and demanding, sending a quiver running through her.

She pulled back, averting her face, gasping out a protest. 'Don't, Macey!'

He didn't even seem to hear. He pressed his face into her neck, kissing her throat fiercely, his cheek hot against her cool skin. A strange, disturbed fluttering began in Clare's stomach as his body began pressing her back against her tumbled pillows. She felt the straps of her nightie snap and then Macey's lips slid down her white breast and panic leapt along her veins.

The raging insistence of his caresses made her go wild with fear. She struggled violently, thrusting him away, hitting him with clenched fists.

'Let me go, stop it!' she moaned in a high, unfamiliar voice.

Breathing thickly, Macey lifted his head to stare at her. She did not know him. He was a stranger in the dangerous moonlight, all the familiar casual warmth stripped from his face.

He sat up away from her, his lean hard body taut. For a moment he didn't speak or move, that heavy breathing gradually slowing, his eyes hidden by shielding lids.

'I'm sorry,' he said at last, his voice harsh. 'I went a little mad.'

She should have left it there. She should have let him apologise and go, but years of affection for him made her stammer, 'Macey, I'm sorry.'

'Sorry?' He almost spat the word at her. 'Don't insult my intelligence, Clare! If I wanted your pity I'd have asked for it years ago.'

Clare hated the coldness in his face, the hardness in his tone. Their long friendship mattered more to her than anything in the world. She could not bear to lose Macey. She had been blind and stupid not to realise that the way she felt towards him was not the way he felt towards her. Macey had shown her something of this in the beginning and she had carefully made it clear she did not want him. She had believed that he had accepted the facts, but obviously she had been very wrong.

She had often wondered why Macey's affairs always broke up so soon. He was a normal male, but his relationships had seemed doomed before they began. Now she looked at him in dismay and realisation. She had become so used to Macey that she hardly saw him as a man any more, and that was a dangerous way to think of any man.

On impulse she sat up to touch his face, looking at him with a deep tenderness. 'Macey,' she began, but he wasn't listening. His blue eyes were fixed on her body. She had forgotten her broken nightgown straps. The gown had slipped again, exposing the high warm swell of her breasts.

Her heart missed a beat at the look in Macey's face. The blue eyes were burning. Clare couldn't move, transfixed by that look.

Macey's features looked stark and powerful in the moonlight, stripped of all thought, all feeling, but one. Clare's throat closed painfully as she recognised it. She froze where she sat, a strange tremor running over her, afraid to move or speak.

Macey half-closed his eyes and a long, hoarse sigh came from him, his lean body shivering as though with cold. Clare stared fixedly at him, trying to speak but almost hypnotised by that look in his face.

When he did move she gave a frightened gasp, but it was too late. His hand trembled as it touched her breast. He stared, the taut hard face openly filled with intent hunger. His head slowly bent forward.

Clare moaned, 'No,' her voice husky, but as his mouth touched her she was seized by a dizzy sense of pleasure. Macey gently pushed her back against the pillows, his head at her breast, his hands shaking as they stroked down her body.

Her heart beat deep inside her body, the rhythm dominating her. Long needles of sexual excitement pierced her. She remembered the sensation and her mind blurred, time shifted, carrying her backwards.

Shock and pain tore through her and she went wild, screaming, and Macey stiffened on her. He looked at her white face, the trembling of her mouth, and his own face hardened and whitened.

'Get your hands off me,' she groaned. 'Don't touch me like that! Oh, God, I feel sick!' She was shaking violently, that terrible panic in her face, and Macey read it with a dark bitterness, his mouth taut.

'My God, what do you think I am?' he bit out harshly. 'Do you think I'd try to force you?' He stopped dead, staring. 'Good God, you do, Clare!'

'Let me alone,' she whispered, covering her face with her hands.

'Clare!' he said again in a low, hoarse voice. 'What the hell put that idea into your head? All right, I went crazy, but surely you know me well enough by now to know I wouldn't do a thing like that to you? I'd rather cut my throat than hurt you.'

She trembled, her fingers pressing against her eyes, and Macey picked up the light continental quilt which lay across the foot of the bed and wrapped it round her quivering shoulders. She huddled in it, shocked and tense, not looking at him.

There was a few moments' silence, then Macey said quite coolly: 'O.K., tell me, Clare. I think I've a shrewd idea now, but wouldn't you like to tell me?'

She was filled with doubt and apprehension. She ached to tell him the truth, pour it all out to him, but she could not bear the idea of seeing his blue eyes fill with contempt as she spoke. He was bound to despise her when he knew how she had let Luke Murry take her that night. Clare knew Macey well enough to know how he looked at the sort of girl who got drunk at parties and went to bed with strangers. Macey might shrug indifferently when he saw a stranger behaving like that—she knew he wouldn't shrug when it was her.

Macey waited, then said curtly: 'It's something to do with Murry, isn't it?'

She kept her hands over her face, shaking her head violently. She couldn't tell him.

He pulled her hands down and his blue eyes were icy. 'Don't lie to me, Clare. My antennae work too well where you're concerned. What did he do to you? Or have I guessed?'

'Nothing,' she said fiercely. 'Nothing.'

'There's something,' Macey retorted, staring at her. 'I know damned well that whatever made you the way you are is bound up with Murry.' He drew a rough breath. 'I could take it when there wasn't anyone else within a million miles of you—but I'm not standing aside while someone like Luke Murry walks off with you.'

'I told you, I can't stand the sight of him,' she denied.

'Do you think I didn't notice the way he looked at you? Either you fancied each other on sight or there's been something between you in the past. One or the other, Clare. Don't tell me I was wrong.'

'Please, Macey, leave it,' she groaned.

'What else have I done for years? I can't take much more of it. I'm warning you, Clare, there's too much between us for me to believe I'm wasting my time.' He swallowed, his voice deepening. 'You care something for me, Clare. I wouldn't have been hanging around all these years if I hadn't hoped that one day I'd find the key to whatever was keeping you packed in ice.'

She softened, her face gentle. 'I'm very fond of you, Macey.'

'Fond!' He threw the word back at her as though it had been a deadly insult. His face darkened with angry blood. 'My God, you try my patience sometimes, Clare. If I thought that was all I had to hope for I'd cut my throat!'

He released her and stood up. 'We're both tired,' he said after a moment, his back to her. 'Go to sleep again, Clare, and no more nightmares. If I come in here again I doubt if I'd have the strength to walk out again.'

He was gone before she had a chance to answer. The quiet closing of the door made her wince.

Tears leapt into her eyes. Macey was the one strong rock in her life and she couldn't bear the thought of losing him. It hurt to face the fact that the warm, platonic relationship she had come to rely on so much had all been a figment of her own imagination. She would never again be able to think of Macey as a brother—because that was not how Macey wanted her to think of him and now she knew it.

How could she have been so blind? Macey had occasionally made one of his ambiguous, dry remarks and she had noted them without ever sitting down to consider what they revealed of his feelings.

Macey had given her hints in the past. Why hadn't she taken them? Had her blindness been deliberate?

Had her subconscious been refusing to face the real truth about how Macey felt?

Just now when she lay there with Macey's dark head moving against her body she had been trembling with a desire she had never thought she would feel again. It shocked and confused her even to remember how she had felt. The traumatic events of that night when she was eighteen had killed all her sexual impulses for so long that she had forgotten she was capable of them. They had flared out of her just now, fierce and sharp and piercingly pleasurable.

The idea flashed through her—was she sexually attracted to Macey after all?

It was so new, so blindingly incredible, that she felt her pulses thud in shock.

She couldn't sleep again. She lay watching the moonlight sliding silently around the room, listening to the whisper of the sea, trying to untangle the confusion of her mind.

When she did fall asleep, she was so tired that she slept well into the morning, untroubled by the brilliant sunshine when it filled the room. She only woke when a plane flew low overhead, startling her out of sleep with a painful jerk.

When she sat up she couldn't imagine for a moment how her nightgown straps had come to break, then hot colour flooded her face as it dawned on her.

She swung out of bed, biting her lip, and took a leisurely shower. There was no sound from Macey. Was he still in bed? Had he managed to sleep last night? Clare was not looking forward to seeing him

again. She had never felt shy and nervous of Macey in
her life, but this morning she knew she was both.

She found Macey in the garden by the pool, wearing brief shorts and a T-shirt, sleeping in the sun like
a lizard.

Clare looked down at him uneasily. His long, lean
body had grace even when he slept and the mouth
which had crushed and coaxed hers last night was tran-
quil in repose.

She plucked some geranium leaves and crumpled
them to release the pungent odour, then scattered them
on his face.

He opened his eyes and his glance slid up to her face.
She caught the wary flicker before he smiled carefully.
'Awake at last, sleeping beauty?'

'I'd say it was a toss-up which of us qualifies for
that,' she said as casually as she could. 'Or were you
just planning your next play with your eyes shut?'

'I work best when I'm sleeping,' said Macey, grin-
ning.

'I won't dispute that,' Clare mocked.

'If you're feeling energetic you can make some
coffee,' Macey told her, stretching his long body
elegantly, his arms above his head.

She went back into the house, gratefully realising
that somehow they had established contact, the casual
surface friendliness she was used to from him. He followed her and lounged talking while she poured the
coffee. The telephone rang ten minutes later and he
answered it, coming back with a slight frown.

'Rowena again. She's read the play and wants me to run over there.'

'I'll stay here,' Clare said at once, tautly. No way was she going to be forced to see Luke Murry again. 'I'm tired and Rowena wants you, not me.'

She half expected Macey to argue, but he looked at her oddly before nodding. 'Right. I shan't be long. If I'm not back for lunch, help yourself.'

'I know where everything is,' she agreed. 'Don't hurry back on my account. Keep Rowena happy!'

When he had gone Clare changed into her bikini and walked out to the pool. The sun was higher now and the air was heavy, scented with roses and spiky lavender which grew along the lower terrace walls. As she was about to dive into the blue water a step made her glance around.

Her face drained of colour as she saw Luke Murry. He was wearing a pale blue denim suit with a dark blue shirt open at the neck. He looked casual, elegant and dangerous.

'Macey will be back in a moment,' she said shakily.

He smiled drily. 'He's expected for lunch with Rowena.' The grey eyes glinted at her, mockery in them, telling her that her lie was silly and as clear as crystal to him.

'I'm not having lunch with you,' Clare bit out.

'Aren't you, Charleston girl?'

She winced and turned away, shivering, her arms wrapped round her body. Any last remaining doubts drained miserably away. He had known all along and been amusing himself, no doubt waiting with enjoyment for the moment of disclosure.

She heard him walk closer and hurriedly dived into the pool. It helped to have something to do, something to keep him at a distance and give her time to think, to review her situation.

He sat down on the lounger and watched her as she swam back and forth, her slender body cutting gracefully through the blue water.

He wasn't going to go away. Clare's heart raced angrily, anxiously. What was she going to do?

At last she couldn't delay the moment any longer. She had half hoped that if she stayed in the pool he might give up and leave, but after a time she realised that the casual calm with which he watched her showed no sign of alteration. He would wait all day if he had to, she sensed. He had the patient, tenacious air, the look of a man who isn't budging.

She climbed out, shaking her hair, and the sheathed grey eyes ran slowly over her without missing a thing. Clare felt her face burning and her temper rising. She picked up the robe she had flung down and slid into it, but by then Luke Murry had made a leisurely inspection of the smooth golden shoulders, the small high breasts only half covered by her wet bikini top, the naked midriff and the soft curve of hip and thigh which was merely accented by the tiny panties. It was a relief, all the same, to hide behind the white towelling robe.

Facing him, she said coldly: 'I mean what I say. I am not having lunch with you.'

'You were lovely when you were eighteen, but now

you're ravishing,' he drawled, leaning back, his hands locked behind his black head. His grey eyes slid over the long brown thighs. 'Quite ravishing,' he said softly, looking up into her angry eyes.

'Get out!' Clare said hoarsely.

He laughed, amusement in his face. 'I'm not going anywhere without you.'

Clare walked past him into the villa and heard him coming after her with alarm. She almost ran to her room and bolted the door. Hurriedly, with trembling hands, she dressed in jeans and a T-shirt. They seemed less dangerous than anything else; at least she felt covered from head to foot. The insolent appraisal of his eyes as she climbed out of the pool had made her feel ill.

When she had slowly blow-dried her hair, she went out and found Luke Murry standing at the shelf holding a row of Macey's books. He was flipping through one and she hated to see it in his hands. He looked over his shoulder at her, eyeing her jeans with a lifted brow.

'That limits our choice of restaurant,' he observed.

'I am not having lunch with you,' Clare informed him stiffly.

Nine years ago he had been the best-looking man she had ever seen. Time hadn't made any difference except to harden his features into even more assurance and give him a silken gloss conferred by money, success and power. But now Clare saw him with mature eyes and she detested the sensual cynicism of his mouth, the self-willed arrogance of his eyes. Those golden looks of his were a hollow mask. The mind under them was far less beautiful.

He smiled confidently. 'I remember you like to play hard to get, Charleston girl, and I don't like it any more now than I did then.'

Her flush made him laugh. 'Did you think I'd forgotten? How could I? You were the loveliest thing I'd ever seen. Why did you run off without letting me know where I could find you? I wanted to get to know you better.'

Sickness clawed at her throat. 'Get out,' she muttered, turning away, her hands clenched at her sides. 'Macey will be back soon.'

'And you don't want him to find me here?' Luke Murry sounded amused, his drawl filled with mockery. 'No, I suppose you wouldn't. You keep your past out of sight, do you? Janson wouldn't much like knowing who shared your bed before him.'

Clare's nerves were being shredded by the tone, the smile, with which he spoke. This was the man who had haunted her for years, who had taught her ineradicable lessons in one night! The charming, passionate stranger who had lured her into his arms had been a mirage. Although she had known that for nine years, she realised illusion clung hard, died hard. She had thought she had none of it left, but as she listened to him now she recognised that there were still trailing filaments of that brief, blind emotion twisting inside her. She despised herself for having let them live so long.

Luke Murry had destroyed her ability to respond

normally to other men. For years she had shrunk from any emotionally dangerous situation. She had been half alive throughout her adult life, and all for a man who wasn't worth looking at twice.

'It's taken me years to find you again,' he murmured behind her. 'I recognised you in that film. It was quite a shock. You'd changed, but I couldn't forget that delectable little body.'

She swallowed, shuddering with disgust. She heard the slurred excitement in his voice and knew what he was thinking, what he was remembering. She hated herself because Luke Murry could remember things like that. She wished she could erase them from his mind.

'Will you please leave?' she asked coldly, swinging to face him. 'I don't want you here when Macey gets back.'

He eyed her speculatively. 'Janson's loyalties are going to be under something of a strain,' he said. 'Rowena asked him over because she wants to give Ray the part Janson promised you.'

Clare stared in disbelief. 'What?'

'Rowena's ruthless where the stage is concerned.' Luke Murry grinned wryly. 'I guess she doesn't much like the idea of competing with you. Ray's a much easier proposition for her.'

Clare was not shocked or surprised, only annoyed. So that was why Rowena had sent for Macey!

'What do you think Janson will do?' Luke Murry asked softly, watching her thoughtful face. 'An interesting thought, isn't it? I suppose it will all depend on how much in love with you he is at the moment.'

'Why have you told me?' Clare asked, her brows furrowed.

'If Janson really gives twopence for you, he won't let Rowena browbeat him into giving Ray that part,' Luke Murry told her. 'I'm sure he's been very useful to you, but you'll find I can be useful too. I have quite a bit of influence in New York. I know everyone in the theatre there.'

She saw the drift of his suggestion and her face hardened. 'Get out!' she snapped.

His eyes held angry heat. As he moved she jumped like a scalded cat, but she was too late to evade him. His hands shot out, catching hold of her shoulders and pulling her towards him. She struggled to avoid his mouth, twisting and sobbing. She could not bear to have him touch her.

She had often wondered what would happen if Luke Murry came back into her life. She had never forgotten the sensitive, warm possession of his lips. As he forced her head round and clamped his mouth over hers, she felt herself falling back through time in trembling, helpless weakness, her hands clutching his arms.

It all happened in a flash of time and was over in a few seconds. The tide which had begun to flow in her halted. Her veins ceased to throb with the pleasure she despised herself for feeling. She stood there and Luke Murry kissed her probingly, sensually, but Clare realised at last that it did not mean a thing to her.

She remembered the heart-throb of the silver screen.

He had kissed her with this dazzling expertise and she had looked at him in amusement as she pushed him away. Luke Murry meant no more to her than that. The illusion he had woven around her had not torn that night—it had lingered in the secret recesses of her mind, making her find all other men dull. Now the illusion faded at last for ever.

Luke Murry lifted his head and gave her a quick, frowning, searching look.

Clare smiled at him, feeling light and free and full of laughter. She saw his eyes grow angry and didn't give a damn.

Softly she said: 'And now that's over, would you mind shoving off, Mr Murry? I don't want to know.'

There was fury in his face, a fury she remembered. Luke Murry did not like being frustrated. He had forced her to submit to him once before and looking into those grey eyes she sensed he was quite capable of doing so again. But as he stepped back towards her there was a movement behind them.

Luke Murry glanced over his shoulder. He was still holding Clare's shoulders in his long hands and their bodies were still very close. Clare looked past him and saw Macey staring fixedly at them.

His face was pale and hard, his blue eyes narrowed in harsh observation of the way they stood, the obvious intimacy of their touching bodies.

Luke Murry released her after a second, very slowly. He turned, an arrogant smile on his mouth, gave Macey a nod which contrived to hold insolence and amusement at the same time.

'Janson! I thought you were lunching with Rowena.'

'I changed my mind,' Macey said through his teeth. There was a dangerous menace to the set of his shoulders and Clare's heart turned over at the look in his face. She had never seen Macey look like that. He was poised for violence, his body taut as wire, his eyes fixed on Luke Murry.

The casual, friendly Macey she had known for years was absent in that harsh face.

Luke saw the threat Macey offered too, and with a careful, measuring glance he began to stroll away.

He's frightened of Macey, Clare thought. Luke Murry was much the same height and build, but there was a force in Macey which made the other man walk clear of him, backing away from the unveiled threat of his tense body.

'Well, see you,' said Luke in a light tone as he walked out of the open french windows, but neither Clare nor Macey answered.

She was staring at Macey, winding a lock of bright hair around one finger like a child, trembling at the look in his eyes.

She knew why Luke Murry had gone so quickly. She knew why he had avoided Macey as he went. She found Macey pretty alarming, too. She met his blue eyes, her stomach cramping at the savagery he wasn't hiding as he looked at her.

CHAPTER FIVE

Huskily she asked: 'You're back early. Why did you leave so soon?'

'Why?' Macey flung that at her in a hard, icy voice. 'Why do you think? When I found he wasn't at Rowena's I knew damned well where I'd find him, so I made an excuse to Rowena and drove back here like a bat out of hell.'

She swallowed. 'I hope you didn't offend Rowena.'

'Damn Rowena!' he bit out. 'What was going on when I arrived?'.

To gain time Clare pushed her hair back from her face, trying to smile. 'What?'

Macey's eyes were like flint. 'Should I apologise for interrupting what was obviously going on?'

'Don't, Macey,' she sighed, making a defeated little gesture. She turned and went out into the garden, staring down over the terraces. Macey came up behind her and stood there silently for a moment.

'You were in his arms,' he said heavily.

'No!'

'Don't lie—I saw you. He'd been kissing you. What came next? If I hadn't been so inopportune, would you be in bed by now?'

'No,' she groaned in sick disgust, her body trembling. He flung her round, his fingers biting into her arm with cruel precision. 'Don't lie to me! I've known you for years, remember. I've never seen you react to any man the way you react to him.' He paused and asked on a low, driven note, 'Are you in love with him?'

'No,' she said, her distaste visible.

Macey relaxed slightly. 'What, then?' he asked. 'There's something. Don't keep lying to me. You've met him before, haven't you?'

She gave a long, deep sigh. 'You came close with that guess of yours, Macey.'

His eyes narrowed on her face. 'And he's the man?' She nodded.

'What happened? You fell for him and he hurt you?'

'Something like that.' She was very aware of the inadequacy of the explanation, irony in her eyes as she looked away. 'I don't want to talk about it. I prefer to forget it.'

'You haven't forgotten it, though,' Macey said harshly. 'Whatever happened between you and that bastard, you've been brooding over it ever since. Are you sure you aren't in love with him?'

'I detest him!'

'All the same, your feelings about him are stronger than any you've ever shown towards any other man. Last night I could feel them even when you weren't looking at him. I've felt that sort of excitement in you before, Clare, but always on stage. You give off a sort of electricity. You vibrate with it. I've often thought you sublimated your sexual energy in your work. I thought that was one explanation for your icy rejection of every man you met—until last night.'

'That wasn't excitement,' Clare bit out. 'That was shock and disgust.'

She should have chosen her words more carefully. Macey picked them up at once. His eyes fixed on her, he asked: 'Disgust? What do you mean, disgust?'

She searched for a way out of telling the truth, her eyes nervous. 'Disgust with myself,' she said at last. 'For having been such a fool as to fall for him.'

Macey's attractive face had a cruel fixity in it as he stared into her eyes.

'I hope you mean that,' he said. 'Why do I get the strong feeling you're lying to me, Clare? Your eyes slide away when I try to read them. Why?'

'You make me feel nervous,' she whispered shakily.

'Nervous!' He laughed shortly.

'You're frightening me,' she added.

His mouth twisted. 'I wouldn't want to do that,' he said on a dry note. 'Eaten yet?'

She shook her head.

'Let's go into Nice,' Macey said. 'I feel like eating out.'

She wondered what Rowena had said to him that morning. Had Luke Murry been telling the truth? Did Rowena want Macey to give the star part in the new play to Ray? She glanced at him sideways and he was staring at the blue sky, his features still taut and hard.

'What did Rowena want?' she asked quietly.

Macey flickered her a glance, his face guarded. 'To talk about the play.'

He wasn't going to tell her, she saw that. Was Macey

torn between his instincts as a friend and his instincts as a playwright who had to choose between having the leading light of the profession or a new name which was not yet fully established? Clare was well known, but Rowena was a legend in her own lifetime. Macey was not going to find it easy to decide what to do—she sympathised with him. She wished she could say so, but she realised she could hardly tell him that Luke Murry had warned her of Rowena's intentions.

Why had Luke done that? He was Rowena's godson and owed her some loyalty, yet he had broken that loyalty when he told Clare what Rowena was plotting.

Macey had to make up his own mind. If she mentioned it to him he would be embarrassed. She would force the issue if she brought it out into the open, and she couldn't do that to Macey. Whatever he decided to do he would do because he felt he must. Clare wanted that part, but it was Macey's play and he had a right to decide what was best for the future success of his own work.

Staring at the twisted olive trees which were scratching like suppliants at the walls, she told herself that Ray would be just as good in the part, anyway. Rowena wasn't making an impossible request. Ray was a very good actress and she was going to get all the help Rowena could give her. Merely from the point of view of having a smooth-running production, Macey would be justified if he agreed to switch the role.

'Well, if we're going to Nice, let's go,' said Macey, getting up suddenly.

In the car Clare stared out at the narrow twisting

road, a little smile on her lips. She was lying to herself when she pretended to be so cool about the part. She wanted it badly. It was her play; she knew that, had known from the first scene. Macey had written it for her. He hadn't needed to tell her so—she had seen it at once.

Ray wasn't having her play! Her chin lifted, a stubborn glint in her green eyes. She looked sideways at Macey. He was still frowning, his face disturbed. Poor Macey! She put a hand over his knee and he jumped and turned his head to look at her.

Clare gave him a slow, teasing little smile. 'Stop glowering.'

'Am I?' His eyes gleamed.

'Like a man contemplating murder,' she said lightly.

'Funny,' he said, 'that's what I am doing.' His smile widened. 'Next time I see him I'll cut his throat!'

Clare looked startled, taken aback. 'Oh!' She had thought he was brooding over Rowena and all the time he had been thinking about Luke Murry.

Macey's eyes narrowed speculatively. 'What did you think I was thinking about?'

'I wasn't sure.'

He looked down at her hand and she took it away, flushing. 'Put it back, I like it,' he said with a quick, amused smile.

Clare gave him a dry glance. 'What did Rowena think of the play?'

His face changed again, the frown returning. 'She liked it,' he said shortly.

'You don't seem overjoyed.' Tell me, Macey, she

thought, watching him. She couldn't let him know she was aware of Rowena's plans, but she wanted Macey to confide in her, although she realised that that would make his decision far more difficult.

'I've got something on my mind.' He said that in a curt, low voice with his head turned away from her.

She sighed. Macey glanced at her and their eyes met. Clare gave him a brief smile, a faint tenderness in her green eyes. Her affection for Macey made her dislike seeing him torn like this—she didn't want to make it any harder for him, if she could help it.

The great white blocks of Nice hotels shimmered in the sunshine. Holidaymakers wandered along in gay, casual clothes, their feet thrust into beach sandals, that leisurely air about them as they contemplated the sea and the crowded restaurants and shops. It took them some time to park the car and then they wandered around, too, in no hurry to find somewhere to eat.

In the end they found a busy, noisy little place where they ate *bouillabaisse*, the rich fish stew which is only to be eaten on the Mediterranean where the particular mixture of fish used in it can be caught daily, fish unlike any Clare had ever eaten in England, with unfamiliar names and exotic appearance. It was fun identifying them, asking the cheerful proprietor the names of those they did not know. The fish were cooked whole in olive oil flavoured with saffron and herbs, but the strong flavour of garlic dominated the dish, and the meal was served in an unusual way too, the fish served in one dish and the strongly flavoured liquid in which it had been cooked served on its own, poured over slices of new

French bread, the whole meal given a final touch by the addition of a bowl of *aioli*, the garlic-flavoured mayonnaise made in and characteristic of the south of France.

Clare and Macey lingered over it, attracting some attention from the other tables which were full of local fishermen whose usual idea of tourists did not fit these new companions. Catching some muttered comments, Macey gave them a cheerful grin and shouted a rude comment in French which made them begin to laugh. Within a quarter of an hour he was exchanging ribald jokes with them. Macey had an amazing ability to meet people on their own ground. He was a chameleon, taking colour from his surroundings. Clare listened and smiled, slapping a couple of the younger men when they grew rather too interested in her. Macey turned and bellowed a crude threat at them. Clare felt her cheeks grow pink at the language, but the fishermen laughed and from then on she was left alone.

It had not been the sort of meal you bolt down and walk away from in a hurry. They stayed for several hours, drinking Pernod, the deceptively strong aniseed drink. It had a tang which hit the bloodstream deceptively and Clare's head began to whirl after two large glasses of it. She was flushed and sleepy when Macey finally steered her back to the car.

'Eating out with you can be an ordeal,' she complained as he slid her into the front seat.

'Didn't you enjoy the *bouillabaisse*?' Macey looked at her in surprise.

'Loved it,' she said drowsily. 'But I didn't love getting my bottom pinched or my knee squeezed.'

He grinned. 'They got my point, though. If they know it's "hands off" they don't need telling twice.'

She lay back, lids lowered. 'All the same, I'll want danger money if we go down there again.'

He laughed at her, patting her knee. 'You shouldn't be so seductive. Can you blame them? In those jeans you're a temptation to any man, especially if his veins are full of Pernod.' He started the car. 'I sometimes think sophistication is a mistake. Those boys saw something they fancied and just reached out for it. It's the basic male instinct and they haven't had to learn to damp it down.'

'Time they did, then,' she said, yawning. 'My God, that Pernod is strong stuff! My head's going round. I feel like going to bed.'

'So do I,' said Macey, and something in his voice made her stiffen, shaken awake at once. She kept her lids down, but she was conscious of him watching her as he drove out of Nice. The sun was very hot on one side of her face, the heat intensified by the glass in the car window. She had lowered the side window and a breeze rushed over her skin. Slowly heat and the effects of the drink made her fall into a light sleep.

She woke up when Macey touched her. Lifting her eyes, blinking, she looked up at him and he smiled at her with tenderness. 'Home, my lady,' he teased.

She struggled out of the car and into the villa, the coolness of the interior striking her so deliciously that she stood there, breathing the quiet air, her eyes closed.

A movement startled her and she opened her eyes and saw Ray standing in the sitting-room, watching her.

'Oh, hello,' she said, shaken into wary watchfulness.

'Hello.' Ray's voice was dry and very cool. The thick cloudy dark hair hung round her face, brushing her slender shoulders. She was wearing a simple white shirt and trousers, her pale skin faintly sun-touched at the throat.

Macey walked in and stopped short. Clare saw the hostility in his face as he took in Ray's presence. She also saw the brief look Ray gave him and almost winced at what she saw in Ray's dark eyes.

'What do you want?' Macey asked so coldly that Clare looked at him in disapproval.

'It's lovely to see her, isn't it? Ray, can I offer you a drink? We've been drinking far too much over lunch, so I'm going to make us some coffee, but we can offer you a choice.'

'Coffee will be fine,' said Ray with her eyes on the floor.

'I'll make it,' Macey muttered.

'No,' Clare said sharply, 'I will. Stay and talk to Ray.'

She went out and closed the door. Why had Ray come; to plead with Macey or to tell him she did not want the part? Clare couldn't guess. Ray was ambitious; she must want the part. But she was in love with Macey and wouldn't want to be forced on him by her aunt. Clare began to make coffee, shrugging. It was none of her business.

She didn't hurry, giving Ray as much time as she could to say whatever she had come to say. When she carried the tray into the sitting-room Macey was shouting. 'Tell her from me she can forget the whole damned thing!'

He cut the words off as Clare came into the room. She caught Ray's glance, her face paler than ever, her lips looking as though she had been biting them.

Clare assumed a cheerful smile. 'Cream, Ray?' She laid the tray down on the coffee table and became very busy with the heavy pot, her head bent as she poured coffee into the small cups.

Macey muttered something and went out of the room. Ray turned as if she was going too, and Clare said quickly: 'Your coffee.'

She felt Ray's hesitation and held out the cup. 'Cream? Sugar?' Ray's slender hand slowly extended.

'I'll take it black,' she said in a low, husky voice.

Clare sat down and gestured to a chair beside her. Ray slowly sat down too.

'What's going on?' Clare asked, sipping her coffee. 'Rowena is up to something, isn't she?'

'He hasn't told you?' Ray looked surprised and then her lips twisted wryly. 'I should have guessed he wouldn't. Macey has a lot of integrity, though Rowena doesn't see that. All her integrity goes into her work. Outside that, she'd sell her own mother if events suggested it. She can't see that Macey isn't cut from her cloth.'

'Drink your coffee before it gets cold,' Clare told her.

Ray looked at her with hostile impatience. 'Don't talk to me as if I were three years old!'

The hostility was born of quite another cause, but Clare let that pass. She drank her own coffee and Ray slowly began to sip hers, her dark head bent.

'Rowena wants Macey to give me the lead,' she said huskily after a moment.

Luke Murry had told the truth. That surprised Clare. She asked herself again why he had told her. What motive had he had?

'I didn't come to try to persuade him,' Ray explained in quick, hasty speech. 'I came to tell him I didn't even want the part. Rowena may not see it, but it's obvious he wrote the part for you. I'm not so desperate for jobs that I need to use blackmail to get them. Rowena had no right to ask him. She hadn't consulted me. I only found out after Macey had gone.'

Clare finished her coffee and poured herself some more, took Ray's cup and poured her another.

'He didn't believe me,' said Ray, and to Clare's horror she saw bright, unshed tears at the back of Ray's eyes. 'He's furious with me.' Her voice was thick and husky.

Clare put the cup into Ray's hands, feeling the way the long thin fingers trembled. She was deeply embarrassed, saddened. She had known for a long time that Ray was in love with Macey, but the pain in the other woman's eyes was disturbing.

Ray suddenly put her untouched cup down and stood. 'Try to get him to believe it,' she said quickly in that deep shaking voice. 'I wouldn't take the part if he offered it to me. I've told Rowena so. She was being kind, but she doesn't realise ...' Breaking off, she turned and almost ran through the open french windows and Clare stared after her with compassionate dismay.

She heard a car start and a few moments later Macey came slowly into the room. Clare looked at him and felt so angry she wanted to hit him.

'Why were you so unkind to her?' she demanded harshly, standing up. 'Macey, don't you realise Ray would never have been a party to Rowena's little plot?'

'She told you?' He looked irritated, his mouth tightening. 'She had no business to tell you anything!'

'Ray wasn't involved in it. She doesn't want the part.'

'I won't be blackmailed.' Macey's skin was flushed, his face hard. 'Whether Ray was involved or not, she was the cause of it. I had a very unpleasant interview with Rowena. I was forced to listen to things I didn't want to hear.'

Clare watched, beginning to guess. What had Rowena made him listen to? Surely to God she hadn't told him pointblank that Ray was in love with him? Surely even Rowena wouldn't have such insensitivity?

'You didn't have to be so brutal to Ray,' she said, under her breath. 'Couldn't you have been kinder, Macey? Surely you realised she was distressed when she found out what Rowena had done? She came to tell you she didn't want the part, yet far from being relieved, you were damned unkind.'

Macey's colour had deepened to an angry, burning red. 'What did you want me to do? Make love to her?'

Clare drew a shaky, shocked breath. 'Macey!'

'Oh, hell,' he muttered, turning on his heel and walking to the window. He stood there, his back to her, running a hand through his hair. 'I'm sorry, that was uncalled for, but if you interfere between people it can be a painful business. Rowena curdled my blood this

morning. Did she think I was so blind I couldn't
see . . .' He broke off, muttering under his breath. 'You
ought to know by now, Clare, that we aren't responsible
for what other people feel. The kindest thing I could
do for Ray was pretend I didn't notice a thing. I've
done that for a long time and I could have slapped
Rowena's face when she kindly told me what I'd known
for a good year.'

She sighed, understanding how he must have felt.
'Rowena should never have said a thing.'

'I don't want Ray's attention,' Macey said hoarsely.
'Any more than you want mine.'

Clare felt her colour running up from her throat to
her hair and bit down on her lips to silence the cry of
shock coming from her.

Macey gave a deep, curt laugh. 'Don't worry. I find
pity intolerable whether it's given or received. I don't
go on my knees begging you for what you can't give
me, and I can't stomach being forced to watch Ray
suffering every time she comes near me.'

'Don't, Macey,' Clare begged. 'Don't talk about her
like that.'

'You started this, I didn't,' he flung back harshly.
'I've had about enough of the subject. First Rowena,
then Ray, then you—my God, is it any wonder I wasn't
all sweetness and light when Ray came here? I haven't
loaded all my feelings on to your back, have I? I've
played it the only way it can be played, as lightly as the
damned comedy it is, because the only way to handle a
scene like that is to do it with as much style and grace
as you can muster.'

Clare felt a bubble of hysterical laughter rising inside her. How typical of Macey to regard even his own emotions as though they were material for a play!

'I've no desire to play the lovesick schoolboy,' he went on roughly, staring out over the green garden, the distant roofs. 'Don't you think there were times when I could have sold my soul to tell you what I felt?'

Her back stiffened, her head lifted. She felt a faint sickness and began to say, 'Macey, please ...'

'If you didn't want to listen to all this you should have minded your own business,' Macey said angrily. 'People should always mind their own business. More trouble is caused in this world by interference than any other single thing.'

'Do you think Ray's grateful to Rowena for what she did?' Clare asked him in quick, soft tones.

Macey sighed deeply. 'No, of course not. Do you think I didn't see how she felt?'

'Then why weren't you kinder?'

'Are you totally insensitive?' Macey's voice rose in a harsh roar. 'She was on the point of tears the whole time. If I'd shown her the slightest kindness, they'd have started, and I couldn't have dealt with it. Ray doesn't have your control, Clare.' His voice lowered, became harsh. 'You walk clear of it all, don't you? Cool and free and self-possessed. In seven years I've only ever seen you react to one man as if you really saw him.'

She did not want to talk about Luke Murry again. 'What did you say to Rowena?' she asked.

'Damn Rowena,' Macey muttered. 'You are in love

with Murry, aren't you, Clare?'

'I hate him,' she said fiercely.

'Hate me like that,' Macey came back with a bitter smile. 'Look at me the way you look at him.'

She met his eyes, trembling. 'You wouldn't want me to loathe and despise you, would you, Macey?'

He stared intently, his face changing.

'You wouldn't want me to feel sick at the thought of you laying so much as a finger on me?'

He stood there, his features taut. 'Why, Clare?' he asked in a low, rough voice. 'Why does he make you feel like that?'

She swung away, shivering. 'Don't, Macey.'

'Tell me,' he asked very quietly. 'How can I fight when I don't know what I'm fighting?'

Her lips were dry. She couldn't bring herself to tell him. It would hurt her more than she could stand if Macey ever looked at her with contempt. Macey waited, breathing carefully, all his attention fixed on her. Clare closed her eyes and then walked out of the room without answering.

CHAPTER SIX

IT wasn't easy for them to re-establish contact. Macey slept for some hours and came into the kitchen while Clare was tossing salad in a large wooden bowl. Looking over her shoulder, she smiled with faint nervousness. He was flushed from sleep, his hair damp where he had showered a moment ago, his body moving with that second-nature grace.

'Rabbit food!' he said lightly. 'And I was hoping for a steak!'

'You can have one,' she assured him. 'Steak and black pepper sauce. I'm having cheese.'

'Slimming again,' commented Macey, smiling.

He stood looking out of the window at the moon which hung right above them, shimmering silvery white in the luminous grape-bloom purple of the sky.

'How about some music?' Macey moved away as though he found the sight of the moon uncomfortable. Clare knew how he felt. She had been looking at it as she worked and wishing it would go away. It brought back thoughts she did not need.

Macey had found a Piaf recording. The throbbing, sultry voice breathed passionately, and Clare looked at the moon and away.

The Piaf murmur stopped dead. Macey put on another record without comment. He was right: that had not been a good choice.

What a stupid, crazy world this is, Clare thought, placing the salad bowl on the table. Macey was right— the only way to treat love was as a comedy. In her case, black farce. She put Macey's tenderised steak on the bars above the smouldering charcoal. Brushing it with butter, she caught the first smoky odour of cooking. Macey wandered back. 'Can I help?'

Clare picked up the large pepper mill and Macey moved back as the black dust drifted down over the steak. 'Not too much, darling.'

'Break an egg for me, please,' she said. 'I'll make the sauce.'

They worked in comparative harmony, talking about a friend who was rehearsing a revival of *The School for Scandal*, commenting on her fellow actors, reminding each other of famous performances. It was a deliberate attempt by both of them to get back to the old footing and it was hard work.

They avoided anything that could touch, however remotely, on more personal subjects. Clare wondered if she should go back to London. It would make it easier for them both.

'We do too many revivals,' Macey said, as he had often said before. 'We should be more adventurous, try out more new plays.'

It was a safe subject. Clare took it up and they fell into a lively argument on the old theme of how far tradition and heritage should be allowed to dominate the theatre. 'We mustn't throw the baby out with the bath water,' said Clare, and Macey fired back, 'Some baby!'

Moving on those well-trodden paths kept them talking, lessened the tension between them, slowly brought them back to a balanced poise. By the time they sat down to eat they were both more relaxed.

After the meal they listened to some music and then both went to bed. Clare slept better than she had the night before, worn out by all the emotional scenes she had had to bear that day.

She awoke feeling refreshed and alert, showered and went out to get some breakfast. Macey was already up, swimming lazily in the pool. Clare waved to him, called, 'Early bird! Caught any worms?'

'Dozens,' he agreed, smiling.

She went back into the kitchen and took her coffee and some fruit out into the sunshine. Macey clambered out of the pool, running his hands through his wet hair. Clare poured him a cup of coffee and he sat down and sipped it, staring at the sky.

Clare ate a peach, drank her coffee and turned over the pages of a French magazine. Macey didn't say a word.

When the telephone went he grimaced at her. 'What's the betting that that's Rowena?' Pulling himself out of the deckchair, he went into the house. Clare poured herself some more coffee.

He came back a few moments later. Clare looked up at him and Macey grinned at her. 'She wants us both this time. The old girl's thrown in her hand.'

Clare shook her head. 'No, you go, Macey. Let her down lightly. Leave me out of it.'

Macey surveyed her. 'That might be tactful,' he agreed after a moment. 'She need never know you were aware what she was up to.'

'Even if she does know, it would be better if I wasn't around this time,' said Clare. 'Let it all blow over.'

He nodded. 'What will you do?'

'Drop me in Nice,' said Clare. 'I'll do some shopping.'

They drove into Nice half an hour later. Macey dropped her on the Promenade des Anglais as she requested, then shot off to Rowena's villa, promising to meet her again later that afternoon.

Clare stood watching people sunbathing on the narrow gravelly beach while the water ran up towards them and fell back like a tired whisper. Yachts zigzagged along the blue waves some way from the shore. A boy on a sailboard capsized, shrieking with laughter, and people looked up to smile as he bobbed about in the sea.

Turning away, Clare waited to cross the road. A car shot past, halted, reversed. She automatically looked in at the driver and stiffened as she recognised him. 'Get in,' he invited softly.

Clare didn't answer. She turned to hurry across the road and heard his car door slam as he climbed out and met her. People looked round to stare curiously.

'Get in, Charleston girl,' he said again, holding her arm. The long fingers were not hurting, but the look in the grey eyes warned her that they could, and would, if she didn't do as he asked.

'Leave me alone,' she muttered, careful to keep her tone low, not wishing to become the centre of a public row which was already attracting interested stares.

'We have to talk.'

'We've got nothing to talk about,' Clare told him, voice rising.

'Maybe I should talk to Janson,' he said.

She stiffened, reading the deliberate note in his voice. 'Blackmail?' She looked at him with biting contempt. 'Get lost! The only thing that will happen if you tell Macey anything is that he'll smash you into the middle of next week.' Her green eyes lashed him. 'You're scared stiff of him. Do you think I didn't notice? You're very brave when it comes to pushing women around, but Macey is out of your class.'

His face ran with angry colour. He looked at her, the handsome features sullen. Clare couldn't imagine what she had ever seen in him. Only an innocent, unsophisticated adolescent could ever be fooled by those dazzling looks. It didn't take much intelligence to see through them.

Luke climbed back into his car and shot away at a terrific pace, his tires screeching on the road. A young gendarme strolling along the promenade halted to stare after him. I hope he's taking the number, Clare thought maliciously. I hope Luke Murry is going to get a summons for dangerous driving.

She wandered away into the town and did her shopping. After that, she had lunch at a quiet little restaurant where the food was good and the surroundings peaceful.

Macey was late. She had to wait for him for ten minutes and when he arrived he apologised, his face wry. 'Rowena kept me talking.'

'Is it settled?'

'More or less. She just dropped the subject of Ray—I think she's finally got the point that I'm not open to that sort of pressure. She talked about the play all the time. She's very enthusiastic.'

'Of course she is,' said Clare, laughing. 'It's a good play.'

Macey smiled. 'Rowena's enthusiasm will make a difference with Phil,' he pointed out. 'He likes a racing certainty before he gambles on anything. Rowena will help sell it to his accountants.' He turned to give her a grin. 'Not to mention you.'

'I'm not in her class.'

'You will be,' he said seriously. 'Rowena's the past—you're the future.'

'Don't go all Delphic on me,' she teased. 'You make my blood run cold!'

They began to drive up the winding mountain road and Macey's hands tightened on the wheel. 'Murry wasn't there,' he said, not looking at her.

Clare didn't say anything.

Macey shot her a look. 'No comment?'

'What comment do you want? I'm not his keeper.'

'You didn't see him?'

'Yes, I've been in bed with him all afternoon,' she said on a note of bitter sarcasm.

Macey flinched and said something under his breath that she pretended not to hear.

'Well, why did you ask?' Clare muttered.

'Sorry,' he said through his teeth.

'So I should think! You're not the Spanish Inquisition.'

Macey turned the car into the drive leading to the villa. 'I told myself I wouldn't even mention his name,' he said brusquely. 'Forget I ever did.'

'Gladly,' said Clare. 'Don't mention it again. If you want it on record, I hate the sound of his name and I don't want to talk about him. Can you remember that, do you think? Or do you need it in writing?'

'Don't, Clare,' muttered Macey, running a hand

through his black hair in a furious movement which spoke of barely controlled rage. 'Can't you see that the very violence with which you react every time his name comes up makes me more aware than ever of something between you?'

'There's nothing between us,' Clare burst out, getting out of the car. She walked away and Macey caught up with her.

'Why won't you tell me what happened in the past?' he asked, halting her with one hand curled round her wrist. 'Can't you see it's driving me out of my mind? I've got to know. It goes round and round my head until I feel like screaming. What happened?'

She looked at him with a white line around her mouth. Macey wasn't going to drop the subject; he was going to dig away until he forced it out of her.

Fierce hot colour flared into her face as she met his insistent eyes. She felt pain eating at her. She was going to have to tell him and then it would all be over between them. Macey would never look at her with tenderness again. She would see his blue eyes change, his face reject her.

Slowly she nodded. 'Very well.'

Macey's hand slackened and dropped. She turned and walked into the house and he watched her. Clare sat down in one of the chairs, her head bent.

'Want a drink?' Macey asked in a clipped voice.

She nodded and he moved to the cabinet. She heard the chink of glass, the smooth movement as he came back to her and pressed a glass into her hand. He had given her whisky. She did not like it much, but she drank it, wincing at the fiery impact as it hit her throat.

Macey stood with his own glass in his hand, sipping the whisky. Clare couldn't look at him.

'I met him at a New Year party when I was eighteen —a friend took me. I'd never drunk much before and I drank far too much without even realising it. By the time I met him I was past knowing what I was doing. We danced and talked, and then he suggested we find a quieter party.'

Macey stiffened. She felt the involuntary movement but didn't look up.

'I was too dumb to understand what he meant, and I went along with him.'

Macey said something under his breath. She didn't catch it, but it sounded violent.

Clare looked into her glass. It was empty. She twisted it in her cold hands.

'Do I have to fill in the gaps?'

'No,' Macey said harshly. 'I think I'd already guessed at most of it. I hoped I was wrong.'

She wished she hadn't drunk all the whisky; she needed some. 'No,' she said bitterly. 'You're far too clever to be wrong, Macey.'

There was a silence for a moment, then Macey said: 'He hurt you.'

She laughed shortly. 'That's an understatement!'

Macey swore hoarsely. 'Why the hell didn't you tell someone?'

'Rape?' she asked in a slow, tired voice. 'How many people would believe me? I went with him of my own accord. And to do him justice, I suppose he thought I was willing, too. He thought I knew what he wanted. How was he to guess I was as thick as a plank?'

Macey walked over to the cabinet and poured himself another drink. Clare held out her glass, still avoiding his eyes. 'I'd like another, please.'

Silently he refilled her glass and she drank some of the whisky. She felt it circulating in her veins a moment later and was grateful for the induced warmth.

'The bastard,' Macey said suddenly, his tone raw. 'I'll kill him! I'll spoil that face of his for life.'

'I'll hold your coat,' said Clare, and laughed shiveringly.

Macey put down his glass and came towards her and she cried: 'No, Macey!' She couldn't bear him to touch her. She felt her skin would shrivel if a man laid a hand on her at the moment. She was shivering violently, her teeth chattering, grating together so that her jaw ached with tension and her face felt alive with nerves, her skin leaping and burning.

Macey stopped a foot away. He stood very still, watching her, and she heard the rough intake of his breath. 'Why on earth didn't you tell me all this long ago?' he asked.

'Do you expect me to boast about it?'

Macey was silent.

'Do you think I like remembering it?' Clare asked with a trembling sigh.

'The other night when you had that nightmare,' Macey said slowly, 'was that what you were dreaming about?'

She nodded without lifting her head.

'And I chose that moment to try to make love to you!' Macey's voice was deep and shaken. 'No wonder you went white! No wonder you've always been so scared of sex. My God, if I ever set eyes on that swine again I'll beat him into flinders!'

She remembered the way he had looked at Luke Murry when he found him here. 'I suspect he guesses that,' she said drily. Luke had been frightened, and no wonder. Macey was enough to frighten anybody when his powerful body was tense with violence.

She heard Macey move and shrank. He knelt beside her, not touching her, speaking in a low, husky voice. 'Maybe you should have told someone about it long ago, darling. Keeping it all locked inside your head was a silly idea. I knew something was eating away at you. I refused to believe it was just that you were emotionally cold and I was right, wasn't I? Shock can play funny tricks on people. If you'd told someone when it first happened you wouldn't have frozen in on yourself for years.'

She registered the tone of his voice and a faint hope stirred inside her. Macey didn't sound disgusted or contemptuous. Her lashes flickered on her cheek. She turned her head to steal a look at him through them and found him watching her, a passionate intensity in his blue eyes. She trembled slightly, shy and confused.

For the first time in their relationship she blushed as Macey looked at her and felt her pulses racing at wrist and throat.

He didn't move, but his eyes narrowed, watching the hot colour stealing up her neck and face.

'Feeling better, darling?' he asked with a sudden husky amusement.

Macey was far too clever, far too quick, not to be able to read her reactions accurately. His mind moved at the speed of light, his grasp of the human mind sensitive and understanding.

'Thank you, Macey,' she whispered.

'For what?' He was surprised, staring at her.

'For being so kind, for understanding.'

She could almost hear the rapid, shrewd thoughts flashing through his head.

'You didn't expect it to make any difference to how I felt about you?'

Her silence answered him. After a pause he said huskily, 'Not a chance, darling. I'm totally hooked on you. Don't you know that? If you had loved Murry and had the faintest chance of being happy with him, I'd have stood aside and let him have you, even though it would have killed me to do it. But knowing what that swine did to you doesn't make me feel any differently about you. Him I'd like to cut into a thousand tiny pieces, but you! How could you think for one moment that it would matter a damn to me, except to make me wish I could have prevented it?'

Her mouth trembled at the deep tenderness of his voice. Macey watched her, then put a tentative hand to her cheek, stroking down the hot curve of her face, his fingers delicate. Every nerve in her skin reacted to the touch of his hand. She was astonished by the force of her own response.

Before she had a chance to react, Macey stood up.

Moving away, he said briskly: 'Now, before we drop the subject for good, am I right in suspecting that Murry has been trying to make it with you again?'

The sickness came back. She nodded silently, her eyes on her clenched hands.

'And you've told him no?'

She looked up then, her face flaring with angry colour. 'I told him to get lost.'

'Then I think the rest is up to me,' said Macey with a savage satisfaction.

Clare felt alarm quiver through her. 'What do you mean?'

'I'm going over there now to sort him out,' Macey said through his teeth. 'I'll teach that swine a lesson he won't forget in a hurry. He'll need plastic surgery when I've finished with him!'

'No, Macey,' she begged, but said it to his back as he walked out with the rapid motion of a tiger scenting blood. Clare leapt to her feet to follow him, her colour going. She ran out of the house, but Macey had already started the car. Before Clare could reach him the engine roared and the car shot away through the gates and turned towards Nice.

Clare stood there, horrified. The best that could happen was that Macey would create a scandal that would cause a great deal of curious, excited talk. At the worst, he might do Luke Murry some serious damage that could get him into trouble with the law. She had never seen Macey look like that. His blue eyes had been alive with violence.

She thought fast, realising what she must do. Hurrying back into the house, she ran to the phone, then realised she did not have Rowena's number. It took her several moments to find the little book into which Macey had written it a few days ago. She dialled the number with shaking hands.

Ray answered, her voice cool when she recognised Clare's voice. She sounded surprised when Clare asked for Luke Murry.

Luke's voice came on the line a moment later. He sounded curt and wary. 'Yes?'

Clare did not waste time on courtesy. 'Macey's on his way over there and he's in a mood to do murder. If I were you, I'd get on the first plane.'

She hung up without waiting to hear his response. She had warned him. She didn't really care what happened to him. All that bothered her was Macey. Clare did not want Macey getting into trouble because of her.

She stood at the window, staring out over the garden. The afternoon was sinking into a deep purple haze. Mist drifted up from the sea, veiling tree and wall, dripping softly from the eaves of the house, but the sky far above it was warm and smooth.

She heard the clock ticking. The regular quiet rhythm beat its way into her head.

How long would it take Macey to drive over there? Please, please, let Luke Murry go before he can arrive, she thought, her eyes closing. God knew what Macey might do. He had looked murderous as he walked out. She had never imagined that Macey could look like that. There was so much in Macey she did not know, for all their years of friendship.

She paced around the room, tense and anxious, listening to the whispering sea, the ticking clock, the far-off rustle of the trees.

She kept looking at the clock and listening. Once or twice she stopped beside the phone and looked at it, her hand moving to snatch it up and then falling again. She couldn't ring that house again. There was going to be enough curiosity aroused by Macey's eruption there, even if Luke Murry had gone.

An hour passed. Macey must have arrived by now. She went into the kitchen and made herself some coffee, drank it black and very strong. Her nerves were prickling, her hands chill. She held the cup between her cold palms and felt the heat of the liquid invading her skin, but her mind stayed tense and disturbed.

When at last she heard the sound of the car she stood up, starting as she realised she had been sitting in the dark without even being aware of it.

She heard Macey's quick step. He halted in the kitchen door, staring at her through the shadows.

'You rang him,' he said flatly.

Clare swallowed. 'What happened?' she asked in a shaking, husky voice.

'He bolted.' Macey switched on the light and she blinked, her face confused. 'Why did you warn him, Clare?' Macey asked, watching her.

'I didn't want you languishing in a French jail,' she said, trying to laugh.

Macey's blue eyes narrowed. 'You weren't protecting him?'

Her eyes flamed with bitterness. 'I wouldn't lift a

finger to save him if he was being trampled to death by elephants,' she said.

Macey relaxed, his long body leaning against the door frame. 'I drove over to the airport, but there was no sign of him. I guess he made off to Paris.'

'Was Rowena surprised when you arrived demanding to see him?' Clare watched him anxiously.

'She wasn't around. I saw Ray.'

Clare nodded, understanding the laconic way he spoke. 'And she told you I'd rung?'

Their eyes met. Macey's face was unreadable. 'She told me.'

Clare looked away. 'I suppose she was curious.'

'Eaten up with it,' Macey said drily. 'Don't worry, I didn't tell her a thing.'

Clare felt suddenly deeply weary. 'I think I'll go to bed,' she murmured, her face feeling cold.

Macey watched her walk away and he didn't say a word. 'Goodnight,' Clare said as she left the kitchen.

'Goodnight, Clare,' Macey said gently.

CHAPTER SEVEN

CLARE felt oddly self-conscious as she joined Macey next morning. Her sleep had been deep and dreamless, the sleep of the mentally and physically exhausted. This morning she felt nervously alive. The sun was high in the sky and the blue water of the pool danced and glittered as she glanced at it.

Macey was in shorts and T-shirt. He was reading a volume of plays and on the low table beside him was a glass of freshly pressed grapefruit juice.

'Slept well?' His voice was casual, his smile as cool as though nothing had happened. Clare marvelled at his ability to snap back into that untroubled frame of mind.

She nodded. 'I think I'll have a swim.' She had put on her white bikini automatically, her mind occupied with the realisation that swimming would give her something to do during the first awkward moments of seeing Macey again.

He made no comment. His glance drifted back to his book and she walked along to the pool, frowning. A faint pique arose in her mind. Macey was too damned cool. Clare found it maddening that she should feel so nervous while he looked as though he hadn't a care in the world.

She dived into the water, her body curving in flight like a swallow. As she surfaced she shot a look towards Macey. His dark head was bent over that book and he seemed unaware of her.

She swam around for a while, then climbed out and wandered back towards him. As she sank into the chair beside him he did look up, smiling casually.

'Want some coffee?'

'Thank you,' said Clare, giving him a tone as light as his own. Macey got up and walked away. She stared at the cloudless sky. She was being ridiculous. Macey was helping her to get over a difficult moment. He was re-establishing their old, casual relationship. She should be grateful to him, instead of feeling irritated. She determined to match his calm manner when he came back.

When he did carry out the coffee, Clare gave him a brilliant smile. 'Marvellous! I'm dying for some coffee.'

'Good,' he said drily, his blue eyes sardonic.

She looked away. No need for her ever to tell Macey what was going on inside her head. He could read her like a book.

He sank down beside her and they drank their coffee while the sun rose higher and the blue sky burnt blindly overhead. Clare smoothed oil into her tanned skin and Macey watched her through half-lowered lids.

'You look like a sun goddess,' he said, smiling.

'Thank you,' Clare returned, her green eyes lowered.

She was very conscious of the colour stealing into her face. Macey had often commented on her looks before and she had laughed at him, throwing back a light remark. Now she couldn't look at him and her own shyness amazed her.

For the rest of that day they did nothing but laze by the pool, taking the occasional swim, reading magazines and French newspapers, eating a light salad in the middle of the day and drinking coffee at intervals. It was a day much like the other days they had spent here, yet it was very different.

'Why don't we have dinner in Nice?' Macey suggested as they moved into the house later.

The sun was low on the horizon. It fell across the blue sea in a golden, glittering pathway. Clare gave Macey a quick glance, shrugging. 'Why don't we?'

'Not much enthusiasm, darling?'

He sounded dry and Clare retorted: 'Too much sun to rouse any enthusiasm for anything.'

He laughed, throwing a quick inspection over her. 'It suits you.'

'How kind,' she bit back, and met the amused blue eyes with a feeling that she was behaving like a spoilt child.

In her own room she looked at herself in the mirror and wondered what had got into her. She had never been so prickly with Macey in the past. Today she had felt jumpy, tense and on edge the whole day. Why?

Wandering into her shower, she stood under the water, her body turning to let the cooling jets wash over her sunheated skin.

The sting of it brought her senses to life and made her mind feel clear and sharp. The languor which the southern sun had induced left her and she stepped out of the shower a few moments later, swathed in a towel, feeling very awake and alive.

She padded across the room and glanced along the rack of dresses. Her eye was caught by one and she reached for it and held it out, frowning. On a mischievous impulse she laid it on the bed, deciding she would wear it. She knew Macey liked it. She had first worn it on an evening they spent together at a film premiere. They had sat in a small party which had included a famous producer whose round, gooseberry eyes had barely left Clare all evening. By the time Macey drove her home she had received a number of whispered, pressing invitations from the man which she had smilingly refused. Macey's usual response to watching men make passes at her was amusement, but on that evening he had been biting in his comments. 'You asked for it.' His eye had swept over her. 'That dress!' He hadn't said much more about the dress, but he hadn't needed to—his eye had said it for him. The famous producer hadn't been the only one to find the dress an incitement.

She took her time getting ready, her pulses jumping nervously every time she heard a movement in the villa. Giving herself a last thorough glance in the mirror, she walked out to join Macey.

He was in the sitting-room, pouring himself a drink, and glanced over his shoulder to ask if she wanted anything.

His dark head stayed in that position for a held second as he stared, his blue eyes shooting over her while he absorbed the impact of the clever little black and gold dress.

It was little more than a sheath for her seductive body, curving round her breasts and clinging to the warm, provocative line of waist, hip and thigh, leaving her long, smooth legs exposed.

Clare suddenly wished she hadn't put it on. It had been a reckless impulse.

She watched Macey's face tighten, his blue eyes narrow. They came back to her face and nervously she said: 'I'll have a Martini, thank you.'

He swung round, nodding. She stared at the powerful line of his body, the wide shoulders and long back. He was wearing a white dinner jacket which fitted perfectly. His black hair brushed the collar, each separate strand vital. Her fingers tingled with a desire to touch one and Clare found herself amazed by that sudden impulse.

He turned to walk across and put her glass into her hand and the cool brush of his fingers sent a wave of heat through her, alarming her even more. She avoided his eyes, sipping her drink, the ice which floated in it touching her dry lips.

The dusk outside was alive with huge, powdery winged moths attracted by the light. They tapped against the closed french windows, fluttering feverishly.

Clare knew exactly how they felt. She had the same sensation inside her chest.

She and Macey weren't saying a word. She was very conscious of that. They had always talked so freely and easily, laughing together, and now they didn't seem to have a thing to say.

She flickered a quick, secret look at him. He wasn't aware of her, his profile abstracted, his eyes on the glass in his hand. Clare stared at the strong, male profile with which she was so familiar but which she felt she was seeing for the first time. Macey's intelligent forehead, heavy-lidded blue eyes, the powerful structure of cheek and jaw, the straight nose and firm mouth—she had seen them all a thousand times and never absorbed them with the intensity she did now.

Suddenly his eyes shot sideways before she could look away. Heat flared in her throat, then she burst out into over-rapid speech. 'Where are we eating? Not *bouillabaisse* again, I hope? I don't think I feel up to coping with all those fishermen tonight.'

Macey's brows shot upwards and a sardonic glimmer brightened his blue eyes. 'No? You look as if you could cope with anything in that dress.'

She burnt instantly, her face flaming. 'What's that supposed to mean?'

'You know what it's supposed to mean,' Macey drawled. 'Don't underestimate me, Clare. Walk near the edge if you like, but don't pretend you don't know what you're doing.'

One of his two-edged lines, she thought. Macey being clever again. She lowered her lashes. 'Don't you like my dress?'

'If I told you what that dress did to me you'd probably scream the place down,' Macey bit out. 'Why do women gamble when they're never prepared to risk it?' He finished his drink, turning away before she could absorb that or react. 'Shall we go?'

Macey was fully aware of the reckless impulse which had made her put on a dress she knew would provoke him. Clare bit her lip as she followed him, feeling very silly. To his departing back she flung: 'I wish you wouldn't walk in and out of my mind as though it was a railway station!'

He laughed under his breath. 'Perhaps it's just as well I do,' he murmured, and she wondered what he meant by that.

As the car slid out of the gates she leaned back and watched the moon softly float up out of the sea. A light mist wreathed it, the silvery radiance spreading downwards and melting across the water.

She had her car window open. A breeze blew lightly in her hair, twisting the golden curls like a caressing finger.

'Where are we going?' she asked Macey dreamily.

His blue eyes thoughtfully surveyed her. 'In that dress, we've very little choice. If I took you into anything but a five-star hotel you'd get eaten alive.'

Clare laughed. 'What makes a five-star hotel different?'

'The men have usually learnt not to grab what they fancy,' Macey drawled. 'I don't say the place won't be crawling with men who'll fancy you on sight, but that would apply wherever I took you. It can get very wearing.'

She opened her eyes. 'What can?'

Macey stared ahead, his profile uninformative. 'Watching men watching you.'

Clare had nothing to say in answer to that. She had never considered what it did to Macey to stand around and watch her with other men.

They were driving down the mountain road. Macey's long hands moved lightly on the wheel, spinning the car with deft precision as they took the bends. Clare always felt nervous on that road. The sheer space on one side of her made her heart crowd into her mouth. She gave the towering, rocky mountain above them a nervous look, not looking downwards.

'Calm down,' said Macey without so much as glancing at her. 'I'm a very safe driver. Any risks I take, I take knowingly and I've always calculated the odds to a hair.'

'That's comforting,' Clare said edgily. 'I'll remember that when I wake up in hospital.'

He laughed. 'You won't be doing that. How many years have I been driving you around? When did I ever have an accident?'

'There's a first time for everything.'

'So there is,' agreed Macey on a drawl that suddenly made the hair rise on the back of her neck.

He had been dropping remarks like that to her for years, the razor-sharp ambiguous comments she had ignored without a qualm, and now she couldn't ignore them any more. Now every time one came she felt her nerves quiver vividly.

She felt feverish, the atmosphere between them screwing up her nerves to a point where she wanted to run for cover. Her hands trembled in her lap and Macey's blue eyes flickered obliquely towards them, observing her reaction with a cool awareness that made her want to scream.

He knew what was happening to her. He was watching her from behind that strong face with the acute observation which made his plays so uncanny.

Clare hated realising that. She was so new to all this —she needed time and space in which to learn to cope with what was growing inside her. The years of emotional withdrawal had ended; she had to recognise that. She was becoming deeply aware of Macey. She had to recognise that, too. But she could not stand having him watch her while she adjusted to her own new emotions. Macey's cool, ironic speculation was far too dangerous. Clare wasn't ready to risk anything. She was afraid of moving out of her self-imposed isolation too rapidly. She might make yet another disastrous mistake. She wanted to go slow, to emerge tentatively, not to rush headlong into an affair with anyone.

They reached the hotel and parked. Clare realised as they walked into the restaurant that, despite Macey's remarks about having no choice, he had already booked a table before they left. They were greeted with flattering smiles by the maître d'hotel and guided to their table, followed by glances from the other clients as they were recognised. Clare was used to being recognised. It did not bother her. She took the seat opposite Macey and consulted her menu, grateful for the cover it afforded her.

'I spoke to Phil on the phone this evening,' he said suddenly, as the waiter took their order and bowed himself away.

Clare was able to look calmly interested as they moved on to this comfortingly familiar ground. 'What did he have to say?'

'He's provisionally scheduled the play for April and I promised to send him the MS at once. He was very interested to hear I'd got Rowena.'

'I'm sure he was,' she returned tartly, and got a grin.

'Well, the news that you were going to play the leading role wasn't so much a surprise to him. I'd already hinted.'

'Before I read it?' Her green eyes were sharp and Macey looked into them with amusement.

'Wicked of me, wasn't it?'

'Typical,' she muttered. 'Have you any ideas on who you'll get to direct?'

He didn't answer, smiling, and she sat forward in surprise. 'You aren't thinking of doing it yourself?'

'Why not?'

Macey was a brilliant director. He had directed several of his own plays in the past, but Clare pondered the wisdom of him directing Rowena in his own play. 'You're far too deeply involved with this one—you and Rowena could come to blows.'

He shrugged. 'I shall be tact itself.'

'You'll need to be!'

'I'm leaning over backwards to keep her happy. She tried to push me around when she wanted your part for Ray, but I think we've settled on an armed truce. Rowena knows now that I'm not the push-over she thought I might be. I think I can manage her now.'

'This I've got to see,' Clare murmured drily.

'Rowena's the sort of female who only backs down when she meets someone she can't bully,' Macey observed.

'Not a kind judgment,' said Clare, watching his cool face.

'Genius is often unlikeable.'

'You ought to know,' she mocked, and got a quick, amused look.

'Thank you, darling, for the vote of confidence.'

It was the sort of teasing, casual exchange of professional smalltalk they were used to and it made Clare feel much easier.

They talked about the play over their meal, their

voices low and confidential, aware of all the attentive ears around them. 'I'll ring Harry tomorrow and get him to book me for the play on a provisional footing,' Clare told Macey.

His blue eyes teased. 'You mean, unless something more interesting comes up?'

'I mean unless Phil backs out for some reason,' she countered, laughing. 'I shan't back out myself.'

Flickering candlelight on their table made Macey's features even more unreadable. He smiled at her suddenly, catching her eye, and a strange little tremor ran down her spine.

Towards the end of their meal the whole room was flung into excited confusion as a new party arrived. Clare looked round idly, hearing the excited whispering, and Macey groaned.

'Wouldn't you know it? Is nowhere safe from her?'

Contrary to all appearances the hubbub and confusion at the door was not the arrival of the Queen of Sheba, merely Rowena making sure that everyone within half a mile knew that she was present. She swept through the restaurant, accompanied by the bowing maître d'hotel, ignoring the stares and adoring looks she was getting on all sides, her bell voice rounding on a peremptory demand that her table be changed. 'Not there, my dear man. I can't sit skulking in corners,' she declared, glancing around the room to find somewhere she preferred.

Her eye fell on Macey and she bore down on him, her hands outstretched majestically, proclaiming in piercing accents: 'Macey, dear boy! Well, this is a delightful surprise.'

Macey rose, taking her hands and kissing them in a graceful homage. Rowena smiled on his bent head, satisfaction in her face, then ran her blue eyes over Clare, inspecting the black and gold dress closely.

'Clare, my dear, how nice to see you again. Very chic, but aren't you thin? Macey must see you eat more.'

Delightful, Clare thought, looking sweetly at her. A pat on the head and a stab in the back all in one breath.

Rowena's party had halted behind her like sheep behind a sheepdog. Ted Kilby grinned at Clare and winked. Ray gave her a brief, tight little smile which obviously hurt.

'You must join us,' Rowena informed them, convinced that they could want nothing else.

Macey smiled. 'How kind!'

'Waiter!' Rowena trumpeted, looking around as though expecting to find him under her feet.

He emerged, bowing, from the throng behind her, and she nodded to him. 'We shall be five, not three. Now, where shall we sit?'

Unhappily the man tried to explain that there wasn't a table free apart from the one she had already rejected. Rowena gave him a honeyed smile. 'You'll manage, I'm sure,' she said.

He did. They were all soon seated at a table from which the unhappy occupants had been evicted while Rowena beamed at them. Clare had to bite her inner lip as the departing guests practically thanked Rowena for her kindness in having them shunted off into a corner.

Rowena's bland assumption that her wishes were all that mattered in the world left Clare breathless. The

way in which the world apparently rushed to agree with
her was quite maddening.

Rowena had no compunction about making it clear
that Macey was the only member of the party in whom
she was interested. She held his attention by the sheer
blinding spell of those blue eyes, never allowing him
to escape her for a moment. She must have been a real
head-turner when she was young, Clare thought; that
devastating arrogance must have knocked men down
and flattened them. She had had a few tales whispered
in her ear about Rowena's youthful escapades. The
patrician beauty of her profile had conquered any number of men. Rowena had never allowed romance to
interrupt her headlong rise to fame, but she had had
her moments.

Catching Ted Kilby's eye, Clare smiled at him, wondering exactly how he felt about his wife. There was
no way of guessing from his face. He wasn't an actor,
but he knew how to guard his mind.

As the evening wore on, people began dancing on
the tiny polished floor in the centre of the room, the
low throb of the music discreet and unintrusive.
Rowena looked at Ray, who was watching the dancers
and tapping her fingers on her knee.

'Macey, my dear, Ray wants to dance,' she boomed.

Clare felt something twist inside her and she averted
her eyes too late from Ray's tense profile. 'No, I . . .'
Ray began huskily, but Macey was already standing up.
He extended his hand without a word.

Clare glanced after them as they walked out on to
the floor. Macey slid his arm round Ray's waist and

laced his fingers through her hand. Ray didn't look at him, her eyes lowered.

They moved into the other dancers. Clare suddenly saw Ray's lips quivering. She found it so painful that she looked away.

There was no way of guessing what was in Macey's mind. He had all the gifts of an actor—a voice which could coax or threaten, a face which deceived and a mind which escaped behind it. He looked polite and casual as he manoeuvred Ray round the floor, but Macey knew the brush of his body against Ray was making her skin so pale it looked dead white, making Ray tremble in his arms as though with a chill.

Looking back over the years of knowing Macey, Clare had to realise that her own instincts were blunt and dull. How many times had Macey leant over her to kiss her briefly? How many times had he dropped one of those dry little comments? How often had they danced together? And nothing of what was going on inside Macey's head had penetrated her realisation!

When Macey guided Ray back to the table Rowena was leaning back with closed eyes, indulging in a brief nap, apparently. Macey shot her an amused look before glancing at Clare, his brows lifted enquiringly, offering her his hand.

Ray sat down and Clare rose, taking Macey's fingers. Every hair on the back of her neck rose up in alarm and excitement. She had danced with Macey dozens of times before, but now she walked into his arms, every muscle rigid, her skin taut, every cell flickering with awareness.

She felt his eyes skimming her averted profile as they danced. He had danced very correctly with Ray, but he had both hands on Clare's waist and she was holding his wide shoulders, her fingertips close to his neck. It was the way they always danced, but never before had the intimacy of their touching bodies made her tremble. Macey's thighs brushed her own and she had to fight not to reveal how that contact affected her. She stared over his shoulder fixedly, the scent of his aftershave in her nostrils.

Macey slid his hands slowly up her back. His fingers touched the bare skin exposed by her daring little dress and she felt them shift restlessly, stroking her flesh. Someone swerved beside them in a dramatic piece of dancing and Macey drew her closer to avoid them. Clare's hands involuntarily moved and she felt her fingers brush his brown throat. The touch of his skin made her jump and her eyes lifted before she had known what she was doing. Macey looked down at her, his lids lowered, the blue eyes hard and enigmatic.

He wasn't showing a thing, and Clare knew she was showing everything. Macey was reading her feelings without difficulty. She was acting with as much lack of control as Ray, she thought in self-distaste.

She drew away, hurriedly pulling herself together. 'I'm tired. Can we go soon?'

'Whenever you like,' Macey drawled, smiling slightly.

That smile bothered her. She suddenly realised that they were going back to a house where they would be alone. They had been alone in it for days and it had never made her feel she was being stretched on a rack before. Her nerves ran with fire and she looked away, swallowing.

They went back to the table and Rowena woke up with a neat careful awareness of where she was, smiling at them majestically. Macey gave a smooth excuse about Clare being tired and Rowena said: 'Tired? The young have no stamina. I'm never tired.'

'You're an example to us all,' Macey assured her, kissing her hand.

'One I notice you don't follow,' Rowena informed him as he rose.

He grinned at her. 'I'm taking notes.'

Ted Kilby murmured something polite as Clare smiled at him. Ray gave her a smile that made Clare feel sick. Macey flung a general glance in their direction before guiding Clare away. Ray's glance followed them and although Clare could not see it, she felt it.

The drive back to the villa was silent. Clare wished it could go on much longer. She wasn't looking forward to arriving. She was tense and strung-up and Macey's occasional sardonic looks told her he knew exactly how she felt.

When he had parked the car he followed her inside and stood looking at her wryly as she mumbled something about feeling sleepy.

She turned away and his hand shot out to capture her wrist. She looked at him in stricken confusion, flushing wildly.

'Shall we get it over with?' Macey asked on a dry note.

'What?' She couldn't meet the blue eyes, her glance averted.

'You know what,' said Macey, tugging on her wrist to pull her towards him. 'You've been palpitating all evening waiting for me to do this, so we might as well have the expected scene. Then you can put it out of your mind and start behaving normally.'

She put up a hand to thrust his wide shoulders back and Macey ran his free arm round her, holding her closer, his hand curving below her breast.

She looked up to say something angrily and their eyes met. Clare felt a peculiar, pulsing excitement start deep inside her.

Her eyes dropped to Macey's lips. She looked at them and knew she had never looked at them before and seen them, not with this concentrated attention. His mouth was so beautifully moulded, hard and controlled yet with a warmth which held her eyes.

He didn't move for a moment, holding her, then his mouth lowered and Clare began to shake at the first brush of it. The hands at his shoulders clenched on his jacket, she yielded to the pressing hand pulling her closer and as she did so Macey's lips parted hers. Hunger flared between them. Clare's hands crept to his neck. Her fingers trembled as they stroked the thick black hair. Her lips quivered and burned as Macey fed demandingly on them.

It was Macey who drew back. Clare was lying against him, her arms round his neck, her body surrendered weakly to the restless caress of his moving hands. When he took hold of her shoulders in a biting grip and held her away from him she looked at him dazedly, flushed and mindless, trembling.

'That's enough,' Macey said thickly, his voice hard.

Clare stared at him, unable for a moment to understand what he had said.

'You'd better get off to bed now,' he told her coolly, his voice clearing slightly.

Clare didn't move. She was still wrapped in the unbelievable pleasure she had felt as Macey kissed her.

'Unless you want me to come with you,' he said derisively, his black brows flickering in a cool mockery.

Her face filled with burning heat. 'Oh,' she said huskily, pulling away from him.

As she turned towards the door Macey murmured, 'Oh, indeed,' very softly. Clare fled from the room and heard him laugh under his breath.

CHAPTER EIGHT

IN her room she sank down on the bed and stared at her own feet, torn between shock and disbelief. She couldn't believe what had just taken place. She hadn't wanted Macey to stop. The heady sweetness of that kiss had only just started and she had wanted more, yet Macey had voluntarily stopped, although she knew he had found it as dizzily exciting as she had. She couldn't be wrong about that. All her newfound instincts had told her that Macey's heart had been thudding as violently as her own, that the hands caressing her had been trembling and that the deep probe of his kiss had been fierce with passion.

Yet he had stopped. Baffled, she lifted her head to stare at the door. Why? Why had he broken off their lovemaking when for the first time she had been responding?

When he drily said that she should go to bed, adding that he might come with her, she had run away in shaken dismay and Macey had laughed. Clare considered that, frowning. What was going on behind that clever face? What was Macey up to?

She couldn't hear a sound. Macey wasn't going to bed. Clare stood up, forcing her thoughts down. She would never sleep while she was in this distracted, disturbed state. She stripped and took a warm shower, her face turned to the needles of water, eyes closed, fighting to keep her mind free of thought.

She wandered around the bedroom in her short towelling robe, trying to pull herself together. Her nightdress lay across the bed, a brief filmy lemon creation. She sighed and picked it up. Dropping her robe, she slid into the nightie and climbed into bed. The light clicked off, and she lay there, listening to the whispering of the trees, hearing no hint of what Macey was doing. Why had he pushed her away? she asked herself again. Why?

Macey knew her so well, that was the trouble. He had picked up her nervous, agitated mood that evening and known what was at the root of it. Clare had been aware of him during every second of the time they spent at dinner. Macey had been dead accurate about that. She had been waiting for him to take her into his arms. Well, Macey had done just as she expected and it had sent her into trembling delirium, yet he had stopped after one kiss.

Clare felt like pounding her fists on the bed. Frustrated, puzzled, irritated, she lay and listened until at last she slept.

She must have been working on the problem all night, because the moment she snapped awake in the golden sunlight the answer flashed into her head.

Macey was refusing to take advantage of her disturbed condition after her confession to him about Luke Murry.

Seeing Luke again had knocked her off balance. She couldn't deny that. From the moment she set eyes on him at Rowena's, she had been flung into emotional turmoil.

It wouldn't be surprising if Macey regarded her changed attitude suspiciously. He wasn't the sort of man who was prepared to take someone on the rebound and he knew very well that Luke Murry had affected her deeply.

A man of less sensitive perception, a man of less intelligence, might have rushed to take what she had been so blatantly offering him last night, but Macey did not want to get her on such spurious grounds. Whatever had happened between them while she was still off balance over Luke Murry would have had no validity once she recovered her reason.

Clever Macey, Clare thought drily, staring at the

sunlight as it ran in liquid splendour over the ceiling.

He had a mind like a knife. It ran ahead of her own, going faster and further than she could follow him, and all without betraying a single thing.

He hadn't said any of this to her last night. He had left it to her to make her own deductions.

In the cold, clear light of morning Clare's mind was working more efficiently than it had last night. Her senses had stopped clamouring. Her brain could consider the problem without the impeding distractions of sexual need.

She couldn't be sure that the way she was feeling was going to last. It had happened too suddenly. After years of seeing Macey all the time, she had become deeply aware of him sexually overnight, and that might pass as rapidly as it had come.

Macey had known that and firmly refused to respond to her beyond that one kiss. Clare found his ability to think and act under such disciplined control very impressive, but a faint pique niggled inside her. Macey might have slipped just a fraction, she thought wryly. He might have felt just the tiniest bit tempted. She wasn't sure she liked the fact that he had been able to resist the temptation she had offered him, even though she was grateful to him now for having done so.

Sliding out of bed, she yawned, her arms stretched over her golden head. A swim, she decided; that was what she needed to wake her up.

Macey was in the pool when she hit it. He grinned at her as she surfaced again, shaking her head free of clinging drops of water.

There was no shadow of reminder of last night in

his face. Clare swam to the far end of the pool, turned and came back, the sun falling over her face and giving it the same golden gleam it was giving to Macey's tanned skin.

Macey climbed out of the water and held out a hand to pull Clare out as she swam towards the side. The effortless strength with which he lifted her made her grin at him. 'Thanks, Tarzan.'

He laughed. 'Impudence,' he mocked, slapping her lightly. 'As Rowena said last night, you're too thin.'

Clare slid him a taunting glance. 'Think so?' Her lashes flickered over her cheeks and she smiled.

Macey's blue eyes narrowed. 'You're asking for trouble,' he warned.

She knew what she was doing. Her green eyes lifted, clear and bland. 'Am I?'

Macey stared into those eyes, his face unreadable. 'Yes,' he said softly, 'you are. Do you know what happens to girls who tease?'

Her mouth curved. 'No. Tell me.'

'I'll show you,' said Macey, and her heart beat a rapid tattoo as he moved.

The next moment she was tumbling back into the water, shrieking, while Macey regarded her with his hands on his hips and a grin curling his mouth. Clare bobbed up, spluttering. 'You rat!' she choked.

'Take it as a warning,' Macey drawled, watching her swim back to the side and laughing, before he turned on his heel and walked into the house. 'I'll get the coffee,' he called over his shoulder as Clare climbed out of the pool.

She flicked her clinging hair back from her face, half

amused, half annoyed. When Macey moved towards her like that she had thought she knew exactly what was in his mind and she had been fiercely excited as his hands reached for her. She should have known better. Macey was always unexpected, and after last night she should have realised that he was determined to turn her down while she was uncertain of her own feelings.

By the time he emerged from the house with the coffee Clare was lying languidly at ease in her chair, her huge green sunglasses veiling her eyes, her body stretched out drying in the sun.

'Lazy creature,' Macey informed her, setting down the tray. 'You can pour.'

She stretched, yawning. Macey sat down, but she knew his blue eyes were observing minutely as she leaned forward to pour the coffee. She was very conscious of his scrutiny and knew that he was perfectly aware of her reaction.

Passing him his cup, she lay back, glad of the shelter of her sunglasses. From behind them she could watch Macey out of the corner of her eye as he drank his coffee and gazed down at the sea below them. His long, lean body shifted, his tanned skin gleaming.

Sexual attraction was an odd thing, Clare mused. How often had she seen Macey like this? And never felt a flicker of awareness! Yet now every move he made kept her eyes riveted to him and made her skin prickle with heated awareness.

She drank her coffee and lay back, her eyes closed. The sun lay in melting warmth across her skin making her feel very sleepy. She slid slowly into a light doze.

Fingers trailed across her bare thigh and she came awake in a rush of consciousness, lifting her head.

Macey eyed her, smiling. 'Hungry? Shall we go in and have some salad?'

She couldn't answer because every nerve in her body was leaping at the memory of that brief touch of his hand. Getting up, she followed him into the house, blinking in the cool shadows of the interior after her sleep in the sun.

Macey talked lightly over the meal about his ideas for direction when they went into rehearsal, admitting wryly that Rowena was going to be his big problem. Clare listened and added a few words here and there without really listening with deep concentration. She was concentrating on something else which absorbed her to the exclusion of everything else. Her eye and ear fed her impressions of Macey at every moment. She was consuming him with her mind, absorbing him into her bloodstream as though he were an element her body had lacked for years and for which it craved.

The graceful movements of that hard male body, the deep notes of his voice, the way his head turned and his brown skin gleamed, the width of his shoulders and the length of his muscular legs—all seemed oddly new and oddly illuminating. How could she have been so blind for so long? How could her senses have been capable of responding to him like this without her even suspecting it?

After her frozen years of emotional deprivation, she was filled with amazement at the realisation that Macey had been around so long without impinging on her consciousness.

Macey had once said that she was packed in ice. Now the ice had cracked across and she was melting with feeling. The thaw was carrying her too far, too fast. She hadn't got a clue how to cope with the rush of eager sensation.

The day wore on as the other days they had spent here had gone. They had come here to relax and that was what they were doing, but although Clare lay about and basked in the sun like a lizard, she was very far from feeling as relaxed as she looked. She had reminded herself scathingly that she was an actress, and surely to God she could act her way through this situation! She was putting on as good a performance as she could now, but she wondered if Macey had any idea that every tiny movement he made sent her blood circulating more rapidly around her body. Was that clever mind of his conscious of the fact that when he leaned over to get a peach from the table, the sight of his long, smooth back made her pulses race? Did she know that the sidelong flick of his eyes turned her heart over?

The sexual attraction to which she had been so blind for so long was doing drastic things to her. She had lain beside him in her briefest bikinis until now and barely been aware of him, but now she was acutely conscious of his glance, her nervous restless eyes unable to meet his when he looked at her.

'Dinner in Nice?' he asked again as they drifted back into the house when the heat of the afternoon faded into dusk. The moths had appeared again, emerging from their daylight slumber. One brushed against Clare's cheek, leaving a faint powdered trail across her skin. She rubbed at it as she looked secretly at Macey.

'Must we?' She did not want to go to Nice again. She wanted to stay here in the villa. She refused to investigate why she felt so disinclined to go out.

Macey's jaw tightened. 'Yes,' he said curtly, 'we must.'

'We could have a steak here,' she suggested.

'We'll go out.'

'I'll do the cooking,' she wheedled softly.

Macey's blue eyes had a sudden hard rage in them. 'And afterwards?' he asked through his teeth. 'What did you plan for me later, Clare?'

A burning flush ran up her face. 'I don't know what you're talking about!'

Macey took a step nearer. His face was suffused with angry blood, his jaw was clenched. 'You know what I'm talking about, Clare.'

She backed, her eyes shifting. 'I don't.'

'The answer's no, Clare. I don't want you using me to get yourself over the shock of seeing Murry again.'

'I was doing nothing of the kind,' she retorted furiously, her body rigid.

'Oh, yes,' he grated, anger making him seem taller and more powerful than ever. 'Do you think I'm too dumb to catch on? You haven't exactly been hiding it. I've been getting smouldering looks from you all day. Well, thanks for the offer, but no. If you want a stud that badly go down into Nice and pick one up!'

Her hand stung across his face in a violent, blind instinct of rage and wounded pride.

Macey's intake of breath was followed immediately by furious movement. He leapt forward, grabbing her arms, holding her like a rigid doll between his hands, his angry face bent towards her.

Clare was shattered by her own instinct of violence. Her nervous, horrified eyes flickered up to his face. His features were hot and taut, his skin showing the mark of her fingers. The white outline turned red as she stared, but it was Macey's eyes that made her shiver as she met them.

The sexual threat in the blue eyes leapt over her. Macey bent her backwards away from him, shaking her. Clare's throat ached with tension.

'You think I'm not dying to give you what you want?' he asked harshly through white lips. 'My God, you stupid little bitch, I didn't close my eyes all night. How could I sleep, knowing you were in the next room and that I could have you if I went in to you?'

'No!' she burst out, shaking, her eyes shifting away from the fixed stare.

'Oh, yes,' Macey said hoarsely. 'You don't need to spell it out for me, Clare. When I kissed you last night you were offering me whatever I wanted.' He looked down at her and his breath caught. 'You're driving me insane,' he muttered. The black head bent and his lips pressed hungrily into her throat, forcing back her head. 'I want you. My God, you know I want you.' His lips were hot and shaking as they slid down her throat to her shoulders and then caressed her breasts where they rose from the tiny bikini cups. 'But not like this,' Macey whispered unsteadily. 'Not like this, Clare.'

The movements of his exploring mouth had sent a wave of heat through her. She closed her eyes involuntarily, swaying limply between his hands, aching to press herself against his body, conscious of the wild intensity of the need driving her.

'Macey,' she breathed weakly, desire making her voice almost inaudible.

Macey's hands clenched, biting into her. The pain of his grip would have made her wince if she had been capable of feeling anything but the fierce, sweet emotions flooding through her.

'Are you listening?' he demanded in a low, harsh voice, shaking her. The rough sound of his breathing outran her own. Clare forced her eyes open, shuddering. The lance of his angry stare thrust through her. Macey watched her, keeping her well away from him, those cruel hands remorselessly rejecting her.

She looked at him dazedly and his face tightened even more. 'For God's sake, snap out of it, Clare,' he bit out. 'You're behaving with the emotional blatancy of a sex-crazy adolescent!'

The drowning excitement fell away and her skin went cold. Shock and self-contempt ran along her nerves and the green eyes widened as she stared back at Macey.

She had never imagined he would ever speak to her like that, his voice like a whiplash, his face set in tight, hard lines.

She dragged herself back from the brink of that wild

fever. Looking down, she swallowed and whispered, 'I'm sorry.'

'So I should think!' Macey sounded even angrier, his voice stinging.

She hated to have him talking to her with that contempt. A sensation of self-disgust was filling every corner of her mind but, contrarily, she was angry with Macey, too, for forcing her to see and recognise what was happening inside her. He had hurt her when he spoke to her like that. She felt very small and stupid. She hated herself. But she felt a strange, confused anger with Macey, for having been witness to her moment of unbalanced emotionalism.

'I'll go and change,' she said stiffly.

Macey did not release her. His fingers were clamped on her upper arms, making it impossible for her to move. 'Give yourself time,' he broke out harshly. 'That swine left you reeling. You're in no state to know what you're doing.'

'Yes,' Clare agreed in a tight little voice.

She could no longer meet his eyes; she was hating herself too much. Macey watched her, waiting, and she sensed that he was hesitating about saying something.

'Clare——' he began.

'Don't say anything else,' Clare interrupted. 'There's nothing that needs saying.'

'Isn't there?' Macey watched her fixedly.

'Please, you're hurting me,' she said, wriggling.

His hands dropped. She walked towards the door, then halted, her back towards him. 'I'm sorry I hit you, Macey.'

He drew a long, hard breath. 'I'm sorry I had to talk to you that way, but I had no choice.'

She bent her head, shivering. 'I understand.'

'Do you?' His voice was low and unsteady.

'I'm grateful to you,' said Clare as lightly as she could. 'I was making a fool of myself.'

'No,' Macey said roughly.

'Oh, yes. You were quite restrained, on the whole. You could have said a lot more.' A sex-crazy adolescent, he had called her, and that was singing inside her head now, making her sick with self-disgust.

'You're right off balance,' he returned quietly. 'After years of being emotionally withdrawn you've suddenly woken up and you don't know what's hit you.'

'You're so clever, Macey,' she threw back in a brittle voice, the faint antagonism unmasked in her voice. 'I can't hide a thing from you, can I? It's disturbing to have someone read everything inside your head at a glance. I don't think I like it.'

'I know you very well, Clare,' he said drily.

'You think you do.' Did he know that at this moment she was hating him? Did he know that she felt she never wanted to set eyes on him again? Macey had rejected her angrily a few moments ago and her own self-contempt didn't lessen the blow that that had dealt at her ego. She felt two inches high every time she remembered the voice he had used to bring her back to her senses, every time she remembered her own drowning excitement as Macey kissed her, the wild need to which she had helplessly surrendered only to have him push her away with icy rejection.

Macey was silent. Clare walked into her own room and closed the door, leaning on it, struggling with her feelings for a long time before she felt able to move again. She wouldn't give him any further cause to look at her with contempt. She had to start acting, so she chose her costume carefully. It always helped to be dressed for a part. Clothes were the mask behind which one hid. Whenever she was thinking herself into a part she spent a long time deciding what to wear. People could be judged by their choice of clothes. It betrayed their character, even if they were totally unaware of it.

When she joined Macey later he was standing by the closed windows, a glass in his hand, staring out into the night. He turned and ran a shrewd, comprehending eye over her. Clare looked back at him coolly, her eyes as unrevealing as she could make them. No way was Macey going to keep walking in and out of her head like that.

'Very charming,' he murmured sardonically.

Macey was an actor, too. He knew the value of costume. He knew what that little cream dress was meant to represent. The modestly scooped neckline, the wrist-length sleeves, meant that Clare was under control again and intended to remain like that,

'Drink?' he asked lightly.

'Martini, thank you.'

He moved to pour it for her and she glanced briefly at his tall, lean body. She was going to have an uphill struggle to keep Macey out of her head. He had too many advantages. He had learnt to read her face at a glance, and that was something which had to change.

In the past she had had nothing to hide from him except one particular thing. Things were very different now.

He turned with her glass and she accepted it, eyes lowered, refusing to let that dangerous awareness of him surface again as he touched her hand.

'I thought we might try Antibes for a change,' he drawled, turning his own glass in his hand. 'We haven't been over there since we arrived.'

'Fine,' said Clare, shrugging.

'There's a little place on the Rue de la Touraque which is highly recommended for its seafood.'

'Sounds lovely.'

'Then we'll try there,' Macey shrugged drily, finishing his drink. He moved to the door. 'Ready?'

They drove down the coastal road in the thick dusk with the sound of the cicadas all around them in the pine trees. Antibes was halfway between Nice and Cannes, across the bay from Nice with the rugged outline of Cap Ferrat marking the turn of the coast opposite.

Once Antibes had been little but two white towers and a few huddled houses sheltering behind town walls. The tourist industry had expanded it far beyond the town walls. On the heights above the bay stood an old fort which had protected the town from invasion. Fort Carré had once held Napoleon prisoner before his name was even known in France. He had waited here during the reign of Robespierre to learn if he was to die on the guillotine. Tourists now filed past the grim cell which was reputed to have held him and stared in fascination, imagining the man fated to rule France sitting in that darkness waiting for death.

The perfume industry dominated the town. Behind it to the north grew acres of flowers grown for their scent. 'We ought to make a special trip out to the flower gardens so that you can see the roses,' Macey observed to her as he turned into the town. They hugged the curve of the bay with the railway station behind them and turned down towards the promenade. People strolled through the lit streets. Cafés spilled over on to the pavements. People laughed and talked at crowded tables.

The Rue de la Touraque was sited just behind the Promenade. Macey parked and waited while Clare joined him. They walked without speaking, each intent on their own thoughts.

Antibes and Juan-les-Pins had slowly merged over the years. Clare glanced along the brilliantly lit sea front and saw the wide, white pathway of the light-house gleaming across the dark water for miles. The hills above were crowded with villas and houses and tonight she felt she needed to be among people.

She was sick of herself, afraid to be alone with Macey. When they walked into the restaurant she was pleased to find it crowded. The last thing in the world she wanted was to be thrust into intimate isolation with Macey tonight.

The harassed waiter looked around him, shrugging. 'No table,' he sighed, spreading his hands. 'You wait?'

Macey ran his eye over the room. He shook his head. 'Never mind, we'll try elsewhere.'

As they turned to leave someone stood up from a table near by and smiled at Clare. 'Please,' he said politely. 'I've almost finished my meal. Won't you join me for a few moments? Then you can have this table.' His dark eyes ran on to Macey, still courteous, his English thickly accented, but very good.

'How kind of you,' she said, smiling at him, glancing at Macey enquiringly.

The Frenchman was alone and, as he had said, was already at the coffee stage. The waiter beamed, pushing them towards the table. 'Good, good,' he said, daring them to refuse.

The Frenchman drew out the chair opposite his own and Clare sat down, smiling at him over her shoulder. 'Thank you.'

He lingered, smiling back, and Macey waited for him to move out of the way so that he, too, could sit down. Clare could feel Macey's silent irritation at being forced to accept a companion at such a moment. Given the invitation, they had had little choice but to accept, though.

When they were all seated, the stranger leant across the table, his tanned skin creased in a friendly, admiring smile.

'To be frank, Miss Barry, I recognised you on sight. I'm delighted to have the honour of your company, even briefly.'

Clare should have guessed, but she had been too pre-occupied to notice anyone looking at her with recognition. She automatically gave him her public smile, her green eyes shimmering between their dark lashes.

'You're very kind.'

He took that as a desire to know his name, apparently. 'Pierre Riardot,' he said quickly, extending his hand.

Clare took it and he lifted her fingers to his lips, giving her a flattering, dark-eyed smile as he kissed them.

Macey watched, his face passive.

'You are on holiday, Miss Barry?' Monsieur Riardot enquired, smiling at her.

'We're staying near Nice,' she admitted.

His glance shot to Macey, curiosity in it. 'Ah,' he murmured, discretion veiling his look a second later. Clare felt herself flush.

'Do you live in Antibes?' She decided he must be around forty. He would have been very attractive a while back. He still was, in fact, and showed no signs of middle age as yet. It was in the mature sophistication of his sun-tanned face that one read his age. Although he occasionally glanced politely at Macey to include him in the conversation he largely concentrated on Clare, his dark eyes flattering.

'I both live and work here,' he agreed. 'I'm a jeweller.' He ran a glance over her, lifting his perfectly shaped dark eyebrows. 'You do not like jewellery, Miss Barry?'

'On the right occasion,' she agreed.

He smiled, those white teeth flashing. 'And tonight is not one of those occasions?'

She felt Macey stirring, his feet shifting under the table. Pierre Riardot noted it, too. He shot him a brief, interrogative glance.

'While you are in the South of France, I should be honoured if you would call at my shop and let me show you some very fine emeralds.' He lifted one hand, smiling. 'No, I am not inviting you to buy them. They are very highly priced and I shall find a buyer, but I cannot imagine any customer who could wear them to the same advantage as yourself. Emeralds are your stones.'

Clare laughed. 'Thank you, I'll remember that.' She wrinkled her nose teasingly at him. 'When I can afford to buy emeralds I'll come and see you.'

'I should be delighted,' he said, inclining his head.

'Your coffee is getting cold,' said Macey, and Clare did not have to look at him to recognise that Macey was annoyed. She had been absorbing that fact over the last few moments. Macey hadn't said a syllable until now, but his lean body had been rigid with silent hostility.

Pierre Riardot slid his dark eyes sideways to look at Macey's hard face. Clare saw his smiling expression fade. He shrugged. 'And I am interrupting your evening with Miss Barry,' he murmured wryly. 'I apologise, monsieur.'

Clare was annoyed with Macey. Even if the man had merely been so kind because he recognised her, Macey should know better than to glare at him like that. Quickly she said, 'Not at all. It's fascinating to have met you. I really must find time to drop in at your shop.'

At once he put a hand into his inside pocket and produced a printed card. 'Any time,' he urged, smiling into her eyes. 'I shall be delighted to see you.'

He stood up, signalling to the waiter. '*L'addition, s'il vous plaît.*' Glancing down at Clare he smiled again. 'It has been enchanting to meet you, Miss Barry. I hope it will not be long before we meet again.'

When he had gone Clare glanced at Macey, meeting the hard glint of the blue eyes defiantly. 'He was very charming.'

'If I'd had to listen to him much longer I'd have poured his cold coffee all over his head,' Macey muttered.

'It was kind of him to offer to share his table!'

'He'd have jumped at the chance of sharing a lot more than that,' Macey said unpleasantly, his lip curling.

'You know what people are like when they recognise you!' It was always happening and she was used to it. Although Macey's name was well known his face was far less instantly recognisable. He was lucky; he didn't need to defend himself against importunate strangers.

'I know what men are like when they look at your figure,' Macey bit out.

'He was being friendly, not leering,' she denied angrily, although she knew very well that those dark eyes had been far more than friendly. Pierre Riardot was too sophisticated to make his appreciation crudely obvious. His eyes had flattered rather than offended.

Macey turned and gave her a brooding stare. 'I know precisely what was in his mind. I've seen it over and over again when men look at you.'

'Then you'll be used to it,' Clare muttered.

'I'll never get used to it,' Macey retorted.

The waiter had appeared beside them, poised to dart away, impatient for their order. Macey curtly gave it without consulting her, knowing her tastes in seafood, and the waiter vanished again, nodding.

They sat in silence waiting for their first course. Macey had ordered a local wine with it. The waiter filled their glasses and rushed off leaving them to eat their chilled melon. Clare had no appetite, but she concentrated on the pale fruit as though she were hungry, her eyes lowered.

The seafood was as excellent as they had been promised it would be—served and cooked as superbly as Clare had ever known before. It might as well have been dry bread. She found it hard to force the food down her throat. Tension kept her aware of every move Macey made, every breath he took.

I ought to take the first plane home, she thought, but it would make it all far too obvious to him. Macey would know immediately what had driven me back to London and I can't bear to have him reading my mind.

She drank some more of the wine and the waiter brought a second bottle. Gradually her wrought-up tension eased as the wine ran through her veins. Her skin grew flushed and her body relaxed. Macey talked about his play and about Rowena and she listened and smiled while she thought about other things.

They took a long time over their coffee. Macey took it black and very strong. 'I've got to drive back to the villa,' he pointed out. 'I shall need a clear head tonight.'

Somehow Clare felt that that was another of Macey's

dry ambiguities. He wasn't looking at her, but she could feel the tension in him which matched her own. Only Macey was capable of smiling wryly at his own emotions, and Clare wasn't. She was being torn apart by feelings she couldn't cope with or contain.

As they got into the car later she felt her nerves flickering with restless excitement. Macey started the engine without looking at her. She sat there beside him, deeply aware of his body moving next to her, the long hands controlling the wheel as he left Antibes and headed for the mountain road above Nice. Macey whistled under his breath as he drove, but Clare could sense the tension mounting in him as it rose in her. Macey was hiding it better, but she knew it was present in him.

The journey seemed to be over before it had started. She walked into the villa with Macey on her heels. He jingled car keys in his hand, still whistling. Clare gave him a quick, uncertain nervous smile.

'Goodnight.'

Macey's mouth twisted in sudden sardonic amusement. 'Stop looking at me as though I might suddenly develop a tail and horns,' he drawled, blue eyes derisive.

'I wasn't.'

'No?' He lifted one brow, the casual stance of his lean body infuriatingly at ease.

'Perhaps I ought to go back to London,' Clare flung angrily. 'We seem to be getting on each other's nerves.'

Macey's eyes narrowed sharply. 'I wondered when we'd come to that.'

She felt her skin flaming. 'Always one move ahead of me, aren't you? I'm sorry to be so obvious.'

'Predictable, not obvious,' he said calmly.

'Don't split hairs!'

'I'm not. I can often guess what you'll do, but that doesn't make you obvious.'

'It merely makes you a mind-reader,' Clare muttered crossly.

He laughed under his breath. 'I suspected that in the present circumstances your reaction might be to run like a rabbit,' he told her in soft tones, his blue eyes mocking.

Her colour deepened and her temper flared. 'Who said I was running like a rabbit? I merely thought that as we seem to be irritating each other it might be best if I left earlier than planned.'

'Do you know your problem, Clare?' His amusement was making her want to hit him, her hands clenched into fists.

'No, but I bet you're going to tell me,' she threw back with unhidden irritation.

'You're an emotional coward,' he told her, watching her with a smile deep in his blue eyes.

'I'm nothing of the sort! I merely thought ...'

'When you're faced with an emotional problem you scoot for the nearest exit,' Macey interrupted in a drawl.

'That's not true!'

'Isn't it?' His sardonic smile underlined the lift of his brows. 'I often wonder how well you know yourself.'

'We can't all be as brilliant as you,' Clare snapped, her green eyes alive with antagonism.

Macey laughed. 'Some of us aren't even in the beginners' class.'

Clare's teeth set. 'Go to hell,' she said, stalking out of the room with her bright head held high.

CHAPTER NINE

IT was impossible to sleep. She was too keyed up, her mind racing like the engine of an overheated car. She showered and slid into her towelling robe, staring at herself in the mirror for minutes on end like someone seeing a reflection they did not expect. The short white robe just reached the top of her golden thighs. The plunge of the lapels left her breasts half visible. Her hair was damp and curling, her face very flushed. She stared at herself blankly for a long time before swinging away in sudden irritation.

She could not go to bed yet; her head wouldn't stop working. She went on impulse to a drawer and found one of her bikinis. She would take a swim in the moonlight. If she was very quiet, Macey wouldn't hear a thing.

She heard the low whisper of music from the sitting-room. The door was closed and she was able to creep out into the garden through the kitchen.

The dark rich sky was glittering with stars. She

stood, listening to the night music of the trees and the distant sea, her eyes fixed on the sky. The garden scents filled her nostrils, all the accumulated heat of the day trapped in the perfume of rose and lavender.

Silently lowering herself into the pool, she shot away at a rapid pace before slowing to a crawl and turning to float on her back, her limbs relaxed, staring up at the star-crowded sky. All day the instincts of sensuality which she had suppressed since she was eighteen had been rioting inside her. She felt like someone who has been shut up inside a revolving washing-machine. Her head was spinning and she was giddy.

She couldn't decide what was happening inside her. How did she really feel about Macey? Her sudden, violent attraction to him had left her shaken and confused.

She couldn't blame him if he refused to believe in her feelings; Clare wasn't sure she believed in them herself. All the same, Macey's biting rejection of her had left bruises on her mind. They had increased her confusion. She felt torn between antagonism and a strange, nagging attraction.

She had to resolve the tangle of her emotions, but she had no idea where to start. After knowing Macey for so long, could she really have begun so abruptly to feel attracted towards him? Was her behaviour really a fit of madness brought on by seeing Luke Murry again? Or was there more to it than a temporary insanity, as Macey obviously believed?

All she knew was that after years of single-mindedly concentrating on her career, she was fiercely, wildly alive. When she realised her own folly in allowing a brief encounter with a vicious, ruthless man to cut her off from life, she had felt like someone being reborn, tingling with life, seeing everything with new eyes.

As she drifted in the warm water her mind drifted, too. She suddenly remembered the night she woke up from nightmare to find Macey in her room. When he lost his head and made love to her so fiercely, she had been jolted by her own response. She had screamed and fought him off, but it had been her own sexual excitement she had been fighting. She had known that even then. The caressing stroke of Macey's hands had made every pulse in her body leap like flame.

That first emotional incident in her life had put her feelings into a deep-freeze, and seeing Luke Murry again had started the thaw, but it had been Macey's passion that night which had completed the process.

Luke Murry had left her with the idea that all men were marauding predators who must be kept at arms' length. She had included in that category every attractive man she met; it had been safer.

Macey had been in a category of his own. She realised now that Macey himself had seen to that. When he realised that any pressure on his part would merely make her shut him out altogether, he had cleverly cloaked his feelings for her and got her to trust and accept him. Macey had made himself so deep a part of her life that she had come to see him almost as asexual, a mind rather than a man.

She wasn't the only one who had been shaken by the appearance of Luke Murry. Macey had seen and recognised her immediate response to the other man, and it had knocked him off balance as much as it had Clare. When he came into her room that night to hold her in his arms in the darkness, Macey had lost his head, driven by dangerous impulses.

Macey had not known exactly what he was watching. He hadn't liked it, whatever it was, and he had reacted as any man would react under threat. He had lost control. She found that slightly comforting. Macey wasn't as far above temptation as all that, after all. He wasn't superhuman. His control was impressive, but it wasn't unbreachable.

Realising all this did not make it any easier for her to be sure of her own emotions.

She had woken out of a dream sleep and felt a violent attraction to the first man she saw afterwards. That was one way of looking at it. Was it the right way?

Or had she always been attracted to Macey and refused to admit it, even to herself?

She was so deep in thought that she didn't hear the french windows opening or hear the step on the tiled surround.

'What the hell are you doing?'

Clare jumped violently and, her head swinging, was so taken aback that water splashed into her mouth and up her nose. Choking, she turned on to her front and swam to the side. Macey stood there, still dressed, watching her with a rigid face.

She climbed out, running her hands through her wet hair. 'I couldn't sleep. It seemed a good idea to take a swim.'

Macey was staring at her half-naked body, his blue

eyes narrowed and fierce, his mouth a hard line.

'No,' he said thickly, 'it wasn't a good idea. Go to bed.'

She froze, her hands at the back of her head, all her muscles tightening as she felt the rake of his blue eyes. 'Don't use that tone to me!'

'Are you deliberately trying to provoke me?' Macey asked harshly.

Clare found the way he was staring at her so disturbing that she lowered her hands, trembling, and moved to pass him.

'And this time stay in your room,' Macey bit out.

Clare stopped dead, infuriated. She glanced over her shoulder, her green eyes angry. 'I'm not a child to be ordered around!'

'Aren't you?' He laughed shortly. 'Funny, that's just what I thought you were.'

Her back stiffened. Prickling with resentment, she looked away, then her slender body turned slowly to face him. She glanced at him through her lashes. 'Is that how you see me, Macey? As a child?'

She saw the hard flush run up his angry face. 'Go to bed, Clare, while I still let you go alone.'

Clare arched her brows. 'Macey!'

He drew a furious breath at the deliberate needling. 'My God, you're asking for trouble!'

'I'm asking to be treated as a responsible adult,' Clare retorted, her eyes flicking up to his face in pointed anger.

For a few seconds Macey didn't speak or move. His eyes held her own intently. Huskily he said: 'Sure?'

At once she retreated before the question, her spine rigid, her face filling with nervous uncertainty. 'Just don't use that tone of voice to me again,' she stammered, her eyes falling from his.

'Where are you going, Clare?' Macey's voice was smooth and soft. She had half turned to go, but his hand caught her arm and held her.

Her lips parted on a frightened, quick-drawn breath. 'I'm ...'

'You're what, Clare?' he drawled. 'Getting cold feet already, by any chance?'

His fingers moved softly, stroking her damp skin, sliding up her arm to her shoulderbone. 'What's the matter, Clare?' He had felt the slow tremor passing over her as his fingers caressed her. 'Cold?'

'Yes,' she lied quickly. 'I'd better go indoors.'

'We'd better both go indoors,' said Macey, watching her.

Clare did not like the way he said that or the way the blue eyes were moving over her.

His hand slid down her back and she gasped: 'I'm wet! Your suit ...'

'Damn my suit,' Macey said huskily. He held her, pressing her closer, looking down into her confused, shifting eyes. 'You want to be treated like an adult. Let's see you behave like one.'

His head came down and at the feel of his mouth against her own Clare's mind shut off. Her eyes shut and she yielded weakly to the hand pressing against her spine, her body trembling. A drowning pleasure flooded over her. She had been waiting for this all day. Her lips parted on an aching sigh and Macey's kiss deepened, taking what she offered with a demand which grew more and more fierce as she submitted to it.

His hand slid slowly up her back. Deftly he unhooked the fastening of her top. Clare was clinging to his mouth, dazed with pleasure. Macey's fingers delicately stroked the white swell of her breast and a languid fever held her.

'Is this what you want?' he asked hoarsely, and Clare couldn't answer except with a trembling sigh, her arms tightening round his neck.

Macey picked her up into his arms, breathing harshly, and carried her into the house. Clare's fingers moved in his thick dark hair, twining sensuously in it. Through almost closed eyes she watched the hard, taut features she had thought she knew so well and the same sense of unfamiliarity came to her, as it had earlier when she looked at herself in the mirror and felt she did not recognise the reflection at all.

Macey, she thought, saying his name inside her head and amazed to find it sounded different.

Macey carried her into her own room. He slammed the door shut behind them with his foot before walking with her to the bed, and the sound of that crash shivered her dazed state.

She woke up, her eyes wide and stricken. She remembered the night when another man had carried her drowsy, yielding body into a dark room, and a terrible stab of panic went through her. She looked at Macey's known, familiar face through the shadows and it was even more alien now.

Macey laid her down on the unruffled bed and knelt to kiss her, but as his face approached Clare was staring at it fixedly, her lips shaking. She knew that hard, set expression. She had seen it before: she had seen that look on Luke Murry's face before he forced her. The stark, driven masculinity had been what warned her that she was in danger.

All expression had gone from Macey's face, too. It was locked in fierce desire, his bones taut under his brown skin.

'No!' she cried out in tones of strangled terror, thrusting him away with both hands on his chest.

Macey froze. He stared into her white face through the darkness. Clare watched him in shock and fear, shaking.

'I can't,' she moaned, swinging away to scramble off the other side of the bed.

Macey's hands hooked her back mercilessly. He was breathing hoarsely as he forced her down on to the bed and wrenched her head round, one hand thrust into her damp little curls to hold her head still.

'You're not tantalising me and getting away with it, you little bitch,' he grated thickly. 'You started this— I'm going to finish it. My God, what do you think I am? I warned you not to play games with me, Clare.'

Her cries of panic were stifled under the relentless force of his mouth. Macey lay on her, his hand sensuously caressing her breasts, her waist, the smooth curve of hip and thigh. He unhooked the tiny clasps which held her briefs together and Clare groaned protestingly, shoving his hand away only to have it return insistently.

She tried to struggle away, but Macey's thigh imprisoned her own and held her down on the bed. His lips refused to relinquish possession of her mouth, bruising the soft curves of it, demanding submission in a series of deep, probing kisses which left her breathless and shuddering.

His hand seductively traced the curve of her naked flesh, caressing, teasing, his fingertips light and warm on her skin. Clare tried not to be aware of what he was doing, but her body was quivering under the impact of those stroking hands.

Slowly she stopped fighting him. She stopped struggling under the imposition of his body and her lips melted under his heated kisses. The stiff rigidity holding her slackened. Macey's fingers shifted and a moment later he had flung off his shirt. His bare chest touched her breasts and Clare moaned under her breath, a dizzying excitement mounting to her head.

Macey took a muffled, sharp breath. 'Clare,' he groaned, his face buried between her breasts.

The nagging ache inside her made her oblivious to everything else. Macey's lips and hands were satisfying a need she hadn't known she felt. Sensuality burned inside her, made her skin so sensitive that the touch of his mouth was like the touch of flame, made her cells dissolve in passion and her mouth dry up with hunger.

'I've got to,' Macey whispered into her throat. 'Tell me you want me to, Clare.'

She went stiff again at once, unable to frame the words that would commit her.

'Clare,' he muttered unsteadily, his mouth searching for a response. 'My darling, you're driving me out of my mind.'

She had softened enough to whisper in a trembling voice: 'I'm frightened.'

'I know,' Macey said on a sigh. He drew back and gently kissed her neck, brushed his lips along her bare damp shoulders. 'I won't hurt you, Clare.' He breathed heavily, his fingers shaking as they touched her smooth, naked flesh. 'I won't force you, I promise. Just relax. Let me love you. I've needed to touch you like this for so long.'

She sensed that the cruel, remorseless sexuality had ebbed. Macey's voice was more familiar; his mind was back in control of his body. A shiver ran through her.

He lifted his head. 'Don't tremble like that,' he said in a low bitter voice. 'I promised I wouldn't make you do anything.'

She lifted both hands to the black head, held it, looking at him with confused shyness. 'Macey darling, I'm sorry. I don't know what's wrong with me.'

He half laughed, his mouth twisting tormentedly. 'Don't you? I wish to God I didn't. How do you think I feel, knowing that all this passion isn't real? Holding you in my arms and feeling you respond but knowing I could be any man?'

'That isn't true!'

'Isn't it? Be honest, Clare. I've always known you were a sensual, physically alive woman, even when you were handing me off every time I came within a foot of you. All your physical responses were dead then. Now they're very much alive—but not for me; for them—

selves. You're aching for fulfilment and you're in too confused a state to know how to control what's going on inside you. If I take you now, in a few short weeks you'll hate the sight of me. Do you think I don't know that?'

'I'd never hate you, Macey,' she said gently, and knew it was true. Macey was almost part of herself. She would never hate him.

He grimaced. 'I think you would, darling. Why do you think I've been almost killing myself to keep you at arms' length? This is no way for me to get you. I'd rather see you married to another man than have a few weeks' satisfaction with you and have you walk away afterwards hating my guts.'

She slid her hands down to cup his face, her palms against his hot cheeks. 'Don't despise me, Macey. I hate to have you looking at me with contempt.'

His face altered, his eyes passionate. 'Contempt? Clare! How can you think that?'

'You looked at me, spoke to me, as if you loathed me earlier.'

His mouth twisted. 'Don't you realise what a temptation you handed me? My God, I've never had such a fight with myself in my life! I was crazy. I had to slap you down hard to stop myself taking you.'

Her colour flooded back, her eyes confused. Macey watched her and laughed under his breath.

'I'd better get out of here while I can, darling. The sight of you is making my temperature shoot through the roof!'

She smiled, her lips shaking. 'Maybe you'd better.'

Leaning forward, quickly she brushed her mouth against his in a light, soft kiss. 'Thank you, Macey.'

'Don't add insult to injury,' he said wryly, standing up.

She watched him walk to the door and open it. He glanced back once, the flick of his blue eyes taking in her pale relaxed body on the bed before he went out.

Clare covered her face with her trembling hands. Now that Macey had gone she was so shaken she felt she was actually ill. The strain of those moments when Macey was out of control had taken their toll. She was exhausted by the effort of keeping him at bay.

He was right, of course; she had driven him to do that. The subconscious drive which was dominating her had flicked him into making love to her only to desert her when Macey became too passionate.

Macey might not despise her, but Clare despised herself. One moment she had been trembling with hungry response, the next she had been torn out of that yielding pleasure to find terror possessing her mind.

They ought to part before something snapped inside Macey's head. Clare had felt strongly a few moments ago that Macey wasn't going to be stopped this time. His body had pulsated with violent sexual energy. He had dragged himself back from the edge, but she was under no illusion about what that effort had cost him.

It wasn't fair to Macey to let this state of affairs go on much longer.

She was angry with herself for her own confusion, for the muddled feelings which were making her behave so selfishly and irrationally. Yet she could not make sense of those tangled emotions or decipher the movements of her own heart.

Macey wasn't Luke Murry. Even when he was violently angry just now he hadn't actually gone on to force her to submit to him. He had half threatened it. She knew the desire had been raging inside him. But Macey had not allowed himself to get completely out of control. He had somehow imposed his own will on the frenzy dominating him and he had gone just now, leaving her, although that last look of his had held a desire which could make her feel weak even in memory.

Clare lay in the tumbled bed watching moonlight fingering the walls, a frown growing on her face.

Was it just that, then? Was she just frightened of the actual moment of possession because of the ruthless violence with which that other man had taken her?

Every time she felt that moment approaching, something went wild inside her head.

What did she actually feel about Macey himself, though? Had she confused her long affection for him with the surfacing of sexual desire inside herself? Was she allowing her passion to turn towards Macey because her buried instincts told her it was safer with him than with some stranger? Luke Murry had been a stranger met by chance in the night and he had wrecked her life. She would not want that happening again. She sensed she would look for security when she next chanced a gamble with love, and who could be safer than a man she had known for years?

She twisted on to her flushed face, the slide of her

naked body on the sheet oddly disturbing.

It was insulting to Macey to feel like that. No wonder his blue eyes had been filled with rage once or twice. He had known what was going on inside her head, no doubt. He had guessed why she had turned to him. She was insulting him by even letting the idea enter her head. No man likes to be regarded as 'safe'. She was tacitly telling Macey that she would let him kiss her, caress her, but he couldn't go any further because she only wanted a safe experiment with him. She did not want to be swept away from her safe little refuge. Macey was right to be angry with her.

Macey wasn't safe at all, she thought drowsily. Those hard blue eyes were the very opposite of safe. Tonight they had bored into her and forced her to see that for herself. She had resisted with panic for a while, but the panic had ebbed.

Clare yawned, her body warm and relaxed now. Macey was—her mind halted, unable to frame the thought. Clare slept.

CHAPTER TEN

THEY were eating their lunch next day when Rowena and Ray arrived. Macey flung down his napkin and grimaced at the ring of the door bell. They knew who had arrived. Rowena's high bell voice rang out too clearly not to be recognised.

'Ray drove me,' she said, sweeping into the room a moment later. 'We felt like visiting. Oh, you're eating!' She somehow made that sound like an accusation and to Clare's fury she found herself apologising, as though she felt guilty to be caught in such a despicable act.

Rowena smiled on her flushed face and turned away to survey the room. 'Charming,' she congratulated them. 'But rather cluttered, isn't it?'

Clare wasn't sure what that meant. She hurriedly began carrying the food away while Macey watched with dry amusement as his lunch vanished from sight half-eaten.

Clare returned from the kitchen in a temper to find Rowena, Ray and Macey out on the terrace. Rowena was now sipping a drink and eyeing the view appraisingly. 'You aren't very convenient for the sea, are you?'

'We've got the pool,' Macey told her.

Rowena gave it a glance. 'Yes,' she agreed doubtfully. 'That must be useful.'

Ray was holding her glass and saying nothing, her dark gaze fixed on the distant sea. She was very elegant in a dusky pink dress which looked expensive and suited her colouring.

Clare was wearing very brief shorts which left her long brown legs exposed. Her halter-necked top was tied at the midriff in a casual bow. The golden expanse of skin gleamed as she moved and Rowena looked at it with smiling distaste.

'Macey, have you thought of act three?' she said, going into the attack with calm disregard of preliminaries. 'That first scene won't do, you know. It hasn't any real heart. It's ... mechanical.' She smiled at him coaxingly. 'Do you know, I think we ought to read the script over together, really get to grips with it, see what we can do to ... smooth out the lumps.'

Macey didn't give a flicker of expression. 'Nothing could please me more, Rowena, when I get back to London. We'll have a session together, smooth out every lump we can find.'

Rowena opened her mouth to protest and Macey went on calmly: 'I've got this rule, you see. I never work on holiday. It doesn't do, don't you agree, to mix business with pleasure? I'm sure you feel the same. When we're all back in London, Rowena. Then we can really turn our minds to it.'

She looked at him, her thin lips tight. 'Just as you say, Macey, of course.'

She was furious, but Macey's unmoved smile defied her. Ray lifted her glass and drank the pale liquid it held. Clare watched her, admiring her looks as she always did.

Undeflected, Rowena was saying: 'In the meantime you could just think about scene one in that third act. What it needs is a little injection of pathos, don't you agree?'

Bells rang in Clare's head. That was one of her big scenes. And Rowena's character wasn't even on stage. Oh, no, Clare thought, she isn't sneaking herself into my scene and stealing it. Little injection of pathos, indeed. What she means is a great big injection of Rowena. Not likely!

'I'll certainly think it over,' Macey returned without showing any particular sign of agreement.

Rowena had to be satisfied with that. She knew when to leave the field of battle. She wandered up the terrace, saying: 'What amazing roses—this is wonderful country for flowers. They really know how to grow them around here.'

Clare glanced after her, half smiling. When she looked back Ray had swivelled towards Macey and was talking to him in a low, husky voice. 'Be patient with her. I know it must be irritating, but she doesn't mean to behave badly.'

Macey looked down at her, the hard curve of his face turned towards Clare. 'Don't worry, Ray. I wouldn't hurt a hair on her head, devil that she is.' He smiled and Clare saw the look in Ray's eyes at that quick, warm smile.

'Thank you,' said Ray, half smiling back, her face flushing.

Macey shifted slightly, his smile going. Clare knew why he looked away. She watched Ray as Macey glanced along the terrace towards Rowena's absent pottering around the flowers. Ray looked at Macey and her dark eyes burned before her lashes drooped to hide the expression.

Clare's throat was hot and tight. My God, she's completely crazy about him, she thought, and at that instant a jagged certainty went through her own mind.

She walked back into the house and continued tidying the room. She heard the others talking outside for another quarter of an hour before Rowena came marching in to say goodbye to her. Ray drifted after her, the sultry dark hair hiding her face. She muttered something polite to Clare and went after her aunt.

Macey saw them off and came back to eye Clare with enquiry. 'You aren't angry with her, are you?'

I'm furious, Clare thought, but then realised that Macey had not meant what she had thought he meant. He was asking her if she was angry with Rowena, and it was Ray who had made her stiff with abrupt jealousy and hostility.

She flushed. 'No, of course not. She's just manoeuvring.' She paused, then added drily, 'But she isn't getting any of my big scenes!'

Macey laughed. 'Don't fret about that—I've no intention of letting her. If Rowena had her way she would unbalance my play. She'll have the part I wrote for her and nothing more. Rowena's incapable of understanding the necessity of interplay between characters, so there's no point in my explaining to her that if she takes a bit from here and a bit from there, the whole play will come crashing down on her head. She's just going to have to do what she's told.'

Clare smiled, a wry little movement of her lips. 'I can't wait for the day we start rehearsal!'

'Fireworks,' Macey agreed, his eyes amused. 'She's a wicked old thing, but I find her exciting to work with —that's how she's managed to climb to the top. Quite apart from being a brilliant actress she has this amazing magnetism. She didn't need looks. Fate unfairly handed her every ace in the pack, didn't it? I should imagine that close contact with her ate up Ray's personality long ago.'

Clare lowered her eyes, feeling again that strange sharp pain. Ray had made her feel pity in the past. She had made her feel uncomfortable. She had never made her feel jealous before. Clare knew Macey didn't find Ray attractive—why should she have felt that odd little pain when she watched Ray looking at him with those passionate, dark eyes?

'If you're still hungry I could get us something else to eat,' she said huskily.

Macey gave her a curious, puzzled look. He had picked up the odd feelings inside her, but he didn't know what to make of them. For once Macey did not have a bird's eye view of what was happening inside her, and Clare was glad about that.

'No, don't bother for me,' he returned. 'Go ahead if you're hungry, though.'

'No,' she said. She couldn't have eaten a thing. She was feeling too tense and confused.

She went out into the garden and lay in the sun. Why had Ray made her feel so angry? Clare knew why. Her pulses were drumming and her ears were deafened with the singing of her own blood.

She had always felt uneasy when she watched Ray looking at Macey in that helpless, unhidden passion, but just now she had felt more than that. She had felt like walking between them, turning to Ray and saying: 'Don't look at him like that. He belongs to me.'

Macey had belonged to her for so long she hadn't

even known it. Ray wouldn't look at him like that if he was married. She thought that the fact that Clare and Macey weren't married or even living together meant that Macey was free.

Macey was not free. Clare stared fixedly at the blue sky, her body tense. One fact was crystal clear now. Only love could explain the agonising lance of jealousy which had thrust through her as she saw Macey smiling at Ray, saw Ray looking at him so passionately. Clare could not bear the idea of Macey with another woman. The idea of him kissing someone else sent waves of violent pain round her body.

She felt restless, frightened, by her own emotions. Her heart was being shaken by a tumult which left her breathless.

Macey came and flung himself down in the lounger beside hers and Clare closed her eyes to disguise the state of her feelings from him. Macey seemed relaxed, so relaxed that very soon she became aware that Macey was actually asleep.

His long body lay in total relaxation, his lips parted, his jawline yielding to sleep. Clare watched him intensely, astonished by the fierce stabbing pleasure it gave her to look at him.

She could not sleep herself. She was physically and mentally exhausted, but her mind was too awake to let go of consciousness. She watched Macey while the afternoon wore on in a golden haze, and he slept like Rip Van Winkle, dead to the world.

Dusk began to fall in a pale thickening pall over sea and sky. Clare crept indoors and began to prepare an evening meal. It was a good half an hour before Macey followed her, yawning, flushed and stretching as he stared at her from the doorway.

'My God, why did you let me sleep like that?'

'You must have been tired,' she commented, putting the finishing touches to their meal.

'I was flat out,' he agreed, and his eyes slid mockingly sideways. 'I haven't been sleeping too well lately.'

Her flush rewarded his teasing.

'You'd better wash. I thought we'd just have cold chicken and salad.'

'Fine,' he agreed, turning to go.

Tonight he wasn't insisting that they go out, and Clare's pulses rattled nervously as she considered that.

'I'll open some wine,' said Macey when he came back a few minutes later. He had taken a quick shower, obviously, his dark hair was damp and stiff. He had changed into jeans and a shirt, too. Clare had done the same earlier before she got the meal.

Macey opened the bottle of white wine which Clare had already placed in the refrigerator. It was just cool enough. Macey filled her glass and sat down, smiling at her across the table.

Clare's flushed face and shifting eyes made him frown suddenly. 'Don't look at me like that,' he accused. 'Stop trembling.'

'I'm not,' she denied, her mouth dry.

Macey's brows shot up. 'No?' He didn't believe her, his face derisive.

She shook her head. 'Taste the chicken, it's delicious.' She was not able to hold his eyes and she couldn't hide that from him.

Macey shrugged and started eating. 'Rowena will come to terms with the facts of life,' he remarked. 'She's just an old piranha, stripping every ounce of flesh she can.'

'And a great actress,' Clare agreed lightly. 'It will be an education just working with her.'

'You can say that again,' Macey agreed drily. 'When you've done a few months with Rowena you'll be proof against anything.'

She pretended to laugh. 'Poor Rowena!' Keeping her eyes on her plate, she added: 'Ray's inherited some of her talent, don't you agree?'

'A pale imitation,' Macey nodded casually.

'No more?'

Macey was finishing his salad. After a moment he said: 'Ray is too repressed.'

Clare laughed flatly. 'I wouldn't say that.' Ray didn't repress anything when Macey was around; she flaunted her feelings for him to see.

'As an actress,' Macey bit out, and Clare looked up, her face very flushed.

'Oh. Of course.'

Macey stared at her and suddenly his blue eyes were narrowing, growing hard and watchful. Clare looked away from the probe of them. She refused to let him see what she was feeling until she was ready. Macey wasn't walking in and out of her head for the rest of her life.

'Sexually she's very far from repressed,' Macey commented, still watching her.

Clare didn't reply to that. Her eyes stayed on her plate.

'She shows everything,' Macey said in a hard cold voice.

'Especially when you're around.'

His hand shot over the table and grappled with her wrist. Clare stood up, startled. He came round the table and looked down into her face, his stare intent.

'O.K., what's going on now?'

'What?' she asked in a husky voice, evading his stare.

'We both know the score where Ray's concerned. I've never given her a shred of encouragement. Why the undertone in that last remark?'

She tugged at her imprisoned wrist. 'You're hurting!'

Macey took her chin in one hand and forced her head up. 'Let me see your eyes, Clare.'

'Why?' she asked furiously. 'I don't want you to see my eyes.'

She shut them defiantly and heard Macey laughing without any real humour.

'I know you don't. That's always a sure sign that you're hiding something. What is it now, Clare? What new problem have you come up with?'

She flared in self-defence, twisting her chin from his hand, 'Why can't you leave me alone?'

Macey stiffened. 'Is that what you want, Clare? Do you want to see the back of me?'

The harsh tone made her body clench in pain. Her eyes flew to his face, wide and anxious. 'No,' she said huskily before she could stop herself.

Macey drew an unsteady breath. 'For God's sake, make up your mind! This on-off policy of yours is sending me haywire. Take me or leave me, Clare, but make it positive soon or I'll do something we'll both regret.'

She lowered her lashes again, trembling, a faint smile curving her mouth. 'Such as?'

Macey was silent so long she looked up at him. He was staring at her fixedly, his blue eyes wild. 'Such as carry you into the bedroom and do what I've been dying to do for seven years.'

Clare hesitated for another few seconds before she burnt her bridges. Dry-mouthed she whispered, 'I love you.'

Macey didn't move. For a second she thought he wasn't even breathing He just stared at her, tense and still, as if he didn't believe his own ears.

His hands came up and closed on her shoulders. 'Say it again. Clare, do you mean it?'

'I love you and yes, I mean it,' she said shakily.

Macey closed his eyes briefly, then his mouth sought and found her own in a fierce, hungry movement. Clare's hand lay against his chest. She heard his heart pounding underneath her palm, striking up into her skin so that she felt the pulse of his blood becoming the pulse of her own. The craving for physical satisfaction became extreme as their kiss deepened. Clare moaned under the demanding pressure of his lips, shuddering with pleasure.

Macey lifted his head at last and looked at her

dazedly, his eyes sleepy. 'My God, I love you,' he whispered. 'I've waited a lifetime. I thought sometimes I'd go crazy. The worst part was knowing you hadn't a clue what you did to me. You'd lean over me and I'd have to look casually unconcerned when every instinct I had was clamouring to grab you.'

She was incredulous at her own stupidity. 'You're too good an actor, darling,' she half smiled.

'My God, I'm the world's best,' Macey agreed modestly.

'The girls you used to tell me about,' Clare said, glancing at him.

Macey grinned. 'Yes?' His blue eyes mocked her.

'Did they exist?'

'Oh, yes, they existed,' Macey said teasingly.

Clare eyed him. 'I see.'

His mouth twisted. 'I had some crazy notion it might wake you up to what you were missing. I'd get so frustrated, I'd have to break away from you, prove to myself that I wasn't incapable of attracting a woman if I tried. But somehow my little flings never worked out. It was a sort of whistling in the dark. I always came back to you. I was totally hooked, I had to come back for my fix. Seeing you was better than nothing at all. Life without you was a very pale colour.'

'I'm sorry, darling,' she whispered, stroking his face, her fingertips tingling at the sensation of feeling his skin beneath them.

'So I should think!' Macey grinned. His smile went and the blue eyes burnt. 'I've been through seven different kinds of hell in the past seven years, Clare.

You're going to have a lot to make up for, darling.'

She looked at him passionately, her green eyes shaken. 'How could you go on loving me? You should have started hating me instead.'

'Oh, I had that, too,' he said, laughing harshly. 'I've cursed you from here to the ends of the earth and then sat like a fool praying for the phone to ring or for a glimpse of you on the other side of a street. I'd have been certified if anyone had known the state of my mind. I despised myself for my lack of will power. I told myself to walk off and forget you and I would walk off and be unable to think of anything else. My God, I loathed myself!'

'And I didn't even guess,' she murmured unsteadily.

'No,' he said drily. 'That was the only thing that kept me from shooting myself; the fact that you had no idea was all that made it possible to cope. I won't pretend I found it easy when you kissed me in your casual way or cuddled up to me on sofas. If you'd known what sort of thoughts were going round my head you'd have run screaming.'

Clare caressed his black head with her fingertips, smiling at him. 'Wicked man!'

Macey turned those blue eyes on her, and her heart raced. 'If we got married right away we could honeymoon here,' he said huskily.

Clare tried not to show him the effect that suggestion had had. 'This is so sudden, Mr Janson,' she murmured lightly, but her smile died as he looked at her and a burning languor began deep inside her.

'My God, Clare, you don't know how badly I want

you,' he whispered as he bent to kiss her.

When he detached himself again he was breathing so unevenly that the sound of his heart almost deafened her as she lay, trembling, against him.

The fierceness of the desire which had burst out in both of them had left them too shaken to speak. Macey's heart took what seemed years to slow from that violent galloping.

His lips brushed her hair. 'What suddenly made up your mind for you?' he asked in that low, husky voice.

'I don't know,' she lied. 'I just looked at you and thought: I love him.'

'Keep thinking it,' Macey told her. 'Never stop, darling. Now I've got you I'll never let you go.' His arms tightened round her. 'Do you know, I had a little game I used to play with myself when I was aching for you. I'd promise myself little rewards for work. If I finished a particular scene that day I'd let myself ring you. It got to be quite a habit and it kept me working when I was worn out. I'll have to think up some new scheme if I can see you all the time.'

'We'll work on that together,' she said, looking at him from under her lashes, a smile teasing him.

Macey's hands tightened on her. 'We will,' he said, his breathing quickening again. 'When will you marry me?'

'Tomorrow,' she promised.

'Reckless!'

'I feel reckless,' she agreed, half seriously. 'I feel as though I had champagne in my veins, not blood.'

'That can be arranged,' he mocked.

'Who needs champagne? I've got you,' she said, and Macey's skin ran with colour, his eyes demanding.

'Shall we honeymoon here?'

'Anywhere,' Clare breathed, melting with passion under the hungry stare of the blue eyes.

'My God, yes,' he said, his voice shaking. 'I wouldn't even notice if it was a bus shelter on Clapham Common.'

'You might not. Others might.'

'Not Clapham Common, then,' he said light-heartedly. 'How about the North Pole?'

'Too cold.'

'The Sahara?'

'Too hot.'

'You're hard to please,' he said, roaring with laughter.

'How about here?' she asked huskily.

His eyes froze on hers, his whole body tense. 'Here, then?'

'And now,' Clare whispered, her skin burning, her green eyes feverish.

Macey drew a long, rough breath. 'My God, I thought you'd never offer,' he said before he picked her up and carried her, smiling, out of the room.

Harlequin Presents Collection

An exciting new series
of early favorites from

Harlequin Presents

This is a golden opportunity
to discover these best-selling beautiful
love stories — available once again
for your reading enjoyment…

because Harlequin understands
how you feel about love.

Harlequin Presents Collection

Available wherever Harlequin books are sold.

GREAT LOVE STORIES NEVER GROW OLD...

Like fine old Wedgwood, great love stories are timeless. The pleasure they bring does not decrease through the years. That's why Harlequin is proud to offer...

HARLEQUIN CLASSIC LIBRARY

Delightful old favorites from our early publishing program!

Each volume, first published more than 15 years ago, is an enchanting story of people in love. Each is beautifully bound in an exquisite Wedgwood-look cover. And all have the Harlequin magic, unchanged through the years!

FREE!

A hardcover Romance Treasury volume containing 3 treasured works of romance by 3 outstanding Harlequin authors...

...as your introduction to Harlequin's Romance Treasury subscription plan!

Romance Treasury

...almost 600 pages of exciting romance reading every month at the low cost of $5.97 a volume!

A wonderful way to collect many of Harlequin's most beautiful love stories, all originally published in the late '60s and early '70s.
Each value-packed volume, bound in a distinctive gold-embossed leatherette case and wrapped in a colorfully illustrated dust jacket, contains...
- 3 full-length novels by 3 world-famous authors of romance fiction
- a unique illustration for every novel
- the elegant touch of a delicate bound-in ribbon bookmark... and much, much more!

Romance Treasury

...for a library of romance you'll treasure forever!

Complete and mail today the FREE gift certificate and subscription reservation on the following page.